MATT BOWER

Acts of Circumstance

by Chris J. Stimson

C.A. Baugh Publishing

Surprise, Arizona, U.S.A.

Copyright © 2016

Cover image provided by

SelfPubBookCovers.com/Revision by C.J. Stimson

This book is a work of fiction. Names, characters, places, and incidents are the product of the author's imagination or are used fictitiously. Any resemblance to actual events, locals or persons, living or dead, is coincidental.

www.cabaughauthor.com

ISBN-10: 0999561839

ISBN-13: 9780999561836

Acknowledgment

To my wife and best friend Caryl.
Whose inspiration as an accomplished author,
and faith in my abilities, gave me what I needed
to start and finish this work.

Author's Introduction

'Acts of Circumstance' was written to introduce the reader to the protagonist Matt Bower, who'll manifest himself over the years as one of the most formidable agents for good the underworld has ever known. Two short episodes inextricably tied together provide the backdrop to show who he is and how he becomes an international agent for the CIA.

At this time in the history of mankind no event or thought is original. Our thoughts have already occurred at some point in time to others somewhere in the world. They're distinct in nature only because they're unique to the one or ones applying or experiencing them, and because they expand in nature as a result of new information. Even so are the stories we write, and read. I hope you like the fast pace of the books and look forward to Bower's future adventures; enjoy!

Episode 1

Speed Trap

A SPEED TRAP IS LIKE A MOUSE TRAP;
IT'S INNOCUOUS UNTIL IT'S YOUR FINGER
THAT GETS SNAPPED INSTEAD OF THE MOUSE.

CJS

P R O L O G U E

"Verdammt! Got me again you lousy piece of trash! I'm going to come back and shoot the hell out of those cameras if it's the last thing I do! That's the fourth time at that intersection in the past year. Well, there goes another two hundred bucks down the drain! Or should I say to the good old City of El Moro. That just ruined my whole life, those SOB's. Last time it was only one mile over the limit and it still cost me the same. Not to mention my insurance premium doubling because of that lousy radar camera. The guy next to me must have gotten it too because he was about to pass me; little consolation though," Karl mumbled to himself as he continued his commute to work. Little did he realize that his name had just been added to an exclusive 'drivers' club; a club that no one has yet to leave, alive.

CHAPTER 1

Matt found himself sitting at his desk wishing he was somewhere else, other than the office. He reached down, lifted up his 'Bahama' shirt and adjusted his concealed Glock '36' so it was more comfortable. When the time had come to obtain a concealed weapons license in Arizona he was amazed at how easy it was. Compared to DC, it was easier than getting a flu shot. Yet violent crime in DC was significantly higher than in Arizona; go figure he thought!

A change to the Glock '36' in the year 2000 was precipitated by an incident back in DC, when he was in a shootout with a murderer he'd pursued for months. Previously the Glock 9mm model '19' had served him well up until that day. In a flash things went from bad to really bad. The 'suspect' decided capture wasn't going to be an option and Matt figured he'd accommodate the scum bag. When the killer leveled his gun at him, Matt's ex-marine instincts took over. He dove to his left, drew the 9mm and put two bullets squarely in the guy's chest, but not before the fugitive got off a few rounds, one of which ricochet off the ground and grazed Matt's leg. When Matt got up and hobbled towards the guy, shock ran thru him. All of a sudden the guy was getting up! The Kevlar vest under his shirt had stopped the bullets, and the fugitive's gun was being leveled at Matt again. Matt reacted with lightning speed and placed two hollow points in the guy's head, which seemed to come apart like a ripe watermelon dropped from a two story building. Since then the 45mm Glock '36' ruled. No more going face to face with a killer like that with only a 9mm in hand. With 155 grains of stopping power in his hollow point bullets, a raging bull would have little chance now!

Matt was born and raised in sunny southern California, in a little town called La Crescenta. Mom and dad parted ways early in their marriage and finally divorced when Matt and his older brother were just beginning puberty. This left them on their own most of the time, making life's 'formative' decisions without too much adult input. He was instinctively a loner, due to his older brother's desire not to have a little tag-along around. So he took up running with kids who were into sports; primarily basketball and football. His physique was made for football, which he seemed to excel in. But his heart was set on basketball. The basketball gods, however, plagued him with mediocre talent; just good enough to make the teams but primarily for the sake of 'warming' the bench! This left him on the fringes of the 'social elite' scene. Not good enough to be asked to the 'upper crust' parties by those who threw them, but good enough to have friends who asked him to go with them. It was a form of acceptance, but not really a fulfilling one.

He had a few 'puppy love' crushes in school, but the girls usually looked on him as a 'friend' instead of a potential love object. Handsome in a rugged way, his social standing was unfulfilling due to his home life and parent's financial standing in the community. With no adult support, the 'popular' kids politely feigned ignorance of his presence. So he grew up not depending on anyone. This honed a mental attitude towards survival; helping him through college, the Marines and later as a police detective.

Matt was not dumb, when he applied himself. Graduation from UCLA was accomplished in three years, with a degree in Criminal Justice; the Marines immediately followed. After his three year stint in the Marines, a move to DC landed a police officer's job, and a wife. After swiftly progressing through the ranks of the force he settled in as a detective in the homicide division. At the end of 17 years, a divorce, and ending with the rank of Captain, it was time to retire and move back to the sand and sun; not the California kind but the Arizona kind!

Turning 43 didn't stop his mind from thinking he was still a kid of 21 when it came to his physical capabilities. He had always kept his 6 foot, 175 lb. body in good shape.

A head full of dark brown hair, green eyes, olive colored complexion, and solid physique radiated an air of confidence to those around him, no matter what the challenge or task. Every day that he was not 'in the field working', without fail, he would do his calisthenics and running, which maintained his stomach's six-pack and a body fat index of ten percent. The only thing in his life that had gotten the best of him was alcohol. The worst part of it though was the fact that he couldn't admit to himself it had gotten as bad as it was. Drinking on the job was not a problem, but once off the clock his hand was filled with a glass. He had high hopes that a life and scenery change would allow him to beat the demon liquor and turn his life around for the better.

As an ex-marine, ex-husband and retired Washington, DC homicide detective, he moved to Phoenix in 2010 to get warm, and dry; less humidity and less booze. His background allowed him to obtain a private investigator's license and open his own independent office, which suited his personality – laid back and independent. His office was Spartan in nature; nothing out of place, everything had a purpose, and void of the comforts of life. He had hired, and fired, a number of office assistants until he finally found one that was willing and able to put up with his 'peculiar' work and personality traits. Her name was Marcy.

Marcy Williams was 23, efficient, loyal, friendly, wrapped in a beautifully proportioned package and newly divorced, for the second time! What else could a PI want for his 'Girl Friday'? She had a six year old daughter named Cindy and they both lived with her mother in a little town called Cave Creek on the outskirts of Phoenix. She was a direct, in your face kind of person; a character trait Matt liked in a front office assistant. When she knew he was going to be in the office she would have coffee ready and the small refrigerator stocked with his favorite things, which meant 'almost' empty. All she expected of her boss was to be paid on time and, of course, a wink or two every now and then. And for Matt, that was an easy task. For this she was always at work on time and always off the clock at 5pm, unless running errands for the office.

Matt's specialty, of course, was homicide cases. But because there were so many 'high profile athletes' running around town with someone else hanging on their arm, other than their wives, the bills were primarily being paid working 'domestic dispute' cases. Murder cases were provided by the sheriff's office, which used him as a consultant from time to time. When the sheriff's budget was fat with extra money they would call him more often than not. And in lean times calls still came in, because he delivered. There had been, over the past two years, times when the FBI had even solicited his help in solving murder cases that seemed unsolvable. That's because he had an 'inner voice' or sixth sense when it came to understanding what pieces of the puzzle where important, and which were not. And because of this he became well known and respected in the criminal justice community locally, and nationally as Matt would soon find out.

The phone rang and Marcy answered it. After a couple of seconds she walked to Matt's office door and leaned in, "It's Doctor Caddell; are you busy?" she smiled, with a cute tip of the head and a wink.

He looked up from the file on his desk, saw the look and composure of Marcy standing there and said, "Tell the doctor the patient is in, then transfer it to my phone and take that silly grin off your face."

"Yes boss, anything else I should tell 'the doctor'", at which time he wadded up a piece of paper and threw it at her saying with an impish frown, "Pick that up will you, and close the door."

Marcy complied, shut the door and immediately transferred the call to his desk.

Doctor Caddell's full name was Ciara Katherine Caddell, whom Matt had been dating on and off for a while. She worked for the County as Assistant Coroner and he was struggling with himself over her. He had 'unintentionally' fallen for Dr. Caddell, but was he ready for another woman in his life; could his psyche take another letdown if it should occur? Would a serious relationship interfere with his ability to stay focused and detached while he tried to solve murders as well as domestic differences? It was too perplexing and complicated for him to think about at this time in his life. He had to focus on keeping his life on track, though for what reason he didn't know. Maybe she could give him one.

Ciara Caddell was 'significantly' beautiful at 5'2" and 105 lbs. She was a redhead, all the way down to her toes! Intelligent, poised and definitely Irish! She was not born in Ireland; her parents had migrated to the U.S. in 1978 when she was just four. She had grown up with her ear bent to the 'brogue' of the Irish so naturally her voice emulated it. She too had taken a ride on the 'marriage' go-round, and had fallen off ten years previously. But she was willing and able to get back on and try again. And this guy Matt seemed like the one she would be able to succeed with, if only she could convince him to see it her way.

"Well hello; what's happening down there in the meat locker?" Matt asked, as he sat back and smiled into the phone.

"Hi. I just finished an autopsy and for some reason I started to get hungry for steak! What are you doing for dinner tonight?"

"Autopsy's makes you hungry for steak? Remind me not to expose my neck around you; I might end up with a couple of fang marks and find myself howling at the moon!"

"Very funny mister hot shot detective. Which reminds me, I called to let you know that the sheriff was just here looking over the most recent victim I just finished with, and he mentioned your name in passing. Thought he might bring you in to consult on the case. Think you're schedule will allow?"

"What happened to the guy?" Matt asked, anxious to get a head start on a real case again.

"Well, since I know you'll be working the case, the victim is a male retired accountant who lived in Sun City, was 76, and has a slight build. All of his internal organs are in good shape for his age, with the exception of his heart, which has the right aorta severed, along with his right carotid artery and larynx. I believe, however, the reason the sheriff is considering bringing you in on this is because this is the twelfth murder victim I've autopsied over the last 84 days; one a week! And it doesn't seem like the sheriff, or the other chief's of police associated with the cases have any idea what's going on."

Matt, at this point, was sitting up in his chair taking notes on a pad of paper he had grabbed from the top drawer of his desk. The first thought that came into his mind when Ciara said one victim a week was 'serial killer'.

"Ciara, could you go back and pull your files on the last five victims and pour over the data to see if there are any consistencies or possible links that might indicate one person is doing this; maybe even two or three working together? I would hope that the sheriff had thought of this, but I have to assume that if he's going to ask me to help he's not convinced that that's the direction he needs to pursue. Have you found anything at this point that might link any of them together?"

"All of them have no one specific indices but some of them do; some were murdered with a similar weapon. Let me pull those and see what I can come up with. How about tonight, at dinner? I'll let you know what I find out."

"Sounds good. Lets meet at Rossini's at 7:30 and I'll treat you to that steak; red and juicy I believe?"

"With the blood still drippin' from it!" Ciara responded in her best Irish brogue. "See you tonight."

CHAPTER 2

Matt was just finishing up at the office. He was about to leave for home and get ready for his meeting with Ciara, when the phone rang. His secretary, Marcy, had left for the day so he picked up the receiver; the sheriff was on the other end. Matt had decided ahead of time that he wouldn't tell the sheriff about discussing the case with Ciara unless he specifically asked. That way the sheriff would be totally candid in his demeanor and with issuing forth information he wanted to disclose to him. He had little doubt that the sheriff would withhold pertinent information from him, but he took few men into his complete confidence and the sheriff was not yet there.

"Matt, this is Sheriff Haynes; have a few minutes to talk?"

"I was just on my way out, but sure, what's on your mind sheriff."

"I was wondering, could you come into my office tomorrow to discuss some work I believe you'd be interested in, say around 10 a.m.?"

"Let me check my calendar, just a second...sure, 10 a.m. is fine - see you then." Matt had made it a point that, whenever he talked on the phone to someone who wanted his services, he would be the one to finish the conversation. He felt it gave him the upper hand whenever the next meeting or conversation with that individual occurred. And in his mind, it worked every time. Evidently a character trait he felt good with.

Matt made it to his apartment at 6:30, just enough time to freshen up and travel to Rossini's to meet Ciara at 7:30 for dinner. His apartment showed that he was a fastidious person; that he cared a great deal about small details and wanted everything to be correct and neat. His clothes were always clean and pressed, his furniture specifically placed, exuding a neat orderliness. Yet, until you got to know him, his personality seemed just the opposite, easygoing, not too fussy or finicky. It almost seemed as if he wore two different hats at times; almost eccentric in a strange way. It's what made it difficult to read or understand him, and he liked it that way.

When Ciara arrived at the restaurant and entered, she saw Matt sitting in a booth over in a corner of the room. He waived to her as he rose to his feet.

"Well, this is a surprise. Usually I'm waiting for you; not you for me."

"I'm turning over a new leaf," he said with a grin, "I don't even have a drink in my hand yet. Can I order something for you?"

"No, I don't think so. Let's see how far we can make it until the urge overcomes us, ok?" Ciara said resolutely, but with a softness in her voice, hoping he wouldn't insist on ordering drinks right off. She knew how much he wanted to quit and she tried to support him in that effort. She truly had feelings for him and wanted him to succeed in kicking the habit. Even though when Matt was drunk you couldn't tell it by looking at him, she wanted his full and undivided attention.

"Ok. Well, how'd your day go at the morgue? There aren't too many men who can ask their dates that, are there?"

Ciara responded to him, with a smirk on her face, "I guess not. And are you considering this meeting a date and not just remuneration for the information I'm giving you?"

"That sounds like a leading question from a prosecutor, or an angler trying to catch a fish. Possibly even a trapper setting a snare?"

"And that sounds like answering a question with a question to evade detection; possibly even commitment. Since all men have an ulterior motive for taking a girl out to dinner, whether it's business or pleasure, I'll cut to the chase and tell you what I found out when I went through the files of those victims we discussed earlier; right after we eat!"

Matt and Ciara ordered their dinners, ate, and dabbled in small talk, with Ciara always bringing the conversation back to their relationship and where it was going.

"When are you going to get serious and make me an honorable woman?"

"I've never questioned that you're already an honorable woman. And with that I think we both need a drink; how about some wine?"

He called the waiter over and told him to bring his best bottle of Chardonnay, just so long as it didn't cost more than fifty dollars. He then looked over at Ciara, who was grinning from ear to ear. "What are you grinning about; I'm on a budget!"

Ciara laughed and said, "That's not it, it's the Chardonnay – it reminded me of an old Irish joke. The Mother Superior at the Convent of St Agnes got all of the nuns together for a little meeting, for something had come up. She said, 'Sisters, we've discovered a case of syphilis in the house!' Whereupon little sister Mary Catherine clasped her hands together joyfully and fell to her knees exclaiming, 'Oh, thank the Lord! We've all been getting so tired of that Chardonnay!'"

Matt looked at Ciara, not knowing whether to laugh or cry. "I know now your inner secrets; you better beware of little green men in lab coats, who are going to make you kiss the blarney stone a thousand times for that joke! Only an Irishman could get off telling that."

Ciara smiled impishly and they both drank a glass of wine together, talking about their daily lives and sharing little secrets about each other. Finally he breached the subject he had been patiently waiting to discuss.

"So, now, what did you find in those files that might be of benefit in solving the cases?"

Ciara reached down for an envelope sticking out of her purse and handed it to Matt, then explained that there were some notes in it that gave more details of what she was about to tell him, so he could refer back to them later when he had more time to digest the information. She then proceeded to explain her findings: "Of the twelve victims that have been murdered in the past twelve weeks, seven of them died as a result of knife wounds, four of them from a single GSW to the head by three different caliber bullets; twenty-two millimeter, thirty-eight millimeter and nine millimeter. And one victim was strangled. Now two of the GSW's were of the same caliber bullet, nine millimeter. However, they came from different barrels so there is no connection indicated there. But, there may be a connection between three of the victims who were shot in the back of the head. The trajectory of the bullets indicate the killer or killers may have been left handed; they entered from the left side and exited thru, or close to, the right eye socket. And all three of the victims shot from behind had gun shot residue, meaning they were shot at close range. The fourth victim was shot in the face, from the immediate front, with no residue indicated. That bullet hit the victim on their right side, smashing the upper lateral cartilage of the nose and passing through the back of the head, exiting the left side of the occipital." She paused for him to respond if he wanted to.

"So you said killer or 'killers'; why not just one?" Matt questioned.

"Because of the three that were shot from behind, two of the bullets were nine millimeter from two different barrels and one was a twenty-two millimeter. So unless one killer used three different guns, more than one suspect is indicated," she explained. "Of course, anything is possible when it comes to murder."

"But, unless one killer was standing close, and on the far left side of one of the three victims shot from behind, all 'possibly' three killers were left handed, correct? And the bullet that hit the other victim in the right side of the face and exited the left side of their occipital would also indicate a left-handed shooter correct? And what would be the probability or percentage of all the killers being left handed?"

"Well let's see," Ciara said seriously, "since we only have data from two years ago relative to the number of murders committed in the US, as well as the number that were committed by left handed suspects, the percentage calculates out to be, approximately...2.6 percent."

"You need to get a life! What do you do in your spare time memorize phone books, or 'The Book of a Million Insignificant Facts'?" Matt said incredulously.

"Well, isn't that a significant number in determining the facts relative to what we have in front of us?"

"Definitely food for thought!" he exclaimed with a faint grin, then asked, "Anything else in your notes that we need to discuss before we have our dessert?"

"Oh, I'm not going to have dessert unless you're inviting me up to your place for whatever you have in mind," Ciara exclaimed, placing her elbows on the table and leaning towards him as she said it.

Matt stared at Ciara for a second, trying to think of what to say, then; "Well smarty pants, set, game, and match! I don't know what to say. Are you hitting on me Doctor?"

"Actually...yes, for the umpteenth time. I'm beginning to think you're either avoiding the inevitable, or you like to play a girl along; which is it? We Irish aren't fence sitters, unless we like the scenery. And even then we like to think we need to own it."

"There's no beating around the bush with you Irish, is there? Once you have your cap set, it's into the wind and away you go! Well Ciara, I care too much for you to let you ruin your life on someone like me. Right now I'm fighting my own demons and until they're for sure dead and gone, I don't want to bring anyone else into my life, especially someone I like and care for very much. I want to keep seeing, and being with you, but I won't ruin your life like I've ruined mine, up to this point. When I'm sure I've worked out a few problems, then I'll be ready to make a commitment again. And I hope you're around when that happens."

Ciara looked at him and pondered for a moment then sat up straight and said, "That sounds fair and honest Matt. Let's go forward then with the business at hand so I can tell you what else I found. But any time you change your mind, you'll need to be the one to let me know, Ok?"

"Thanks Ciara, I will. I value our relationship and never want to do anything that would jeopardize it."

"Ok then, let's proceed with my findings. Do you remember when I called today and told you the guy I was working on had his right carotid and right aorta severed?

Well, from the way the blade entered and exited, it too indicates the murderer used his left hand and was standing behind the victim. Of the seven other victims who were killed with a knife, five of them had wounds consistent with a left-handed person. I can also tell you that all of the knife wounds on all eight victims were made with the same or similar blade type. And most of the cuts included a small bruise mark, possibly from where the knife meets the handle. This would indicate the killer plunged the knife so hard into the victims that it forced the bolster up against the body, making a bruise. Finally, the one victim that was not shot or killed by a knife was strangled with a rope, which caused the asphyxiation. It was an eight-year old boy, and the rope used was still around his neck. The knot was a slip knot, which also indicated by the way the rope crossed over itself, that it was tied by a left handed person. That's about it for now. If I find anything else that would help, I'll let you know."

"So, unless we have a gang of left handed killers, we're looking for a single individual/possibly two, that are left handed. Someone the victims probably trusted enough to allow to get up close and personal, hence the gun residue and bruise marks from a knife that was plunged hard against the body. Is there any connection between the little boy and the other victims?"

"Yes. The boy was the son of one of the victims. He was found in one of the bedrooms of the house where his mother was killed, possibly collateral damage. I can't figure out why he too wasn't killed the way his mother was, with a knife. It looks like he was in his bed sleeping when the noose was placed around his neck; definitely a cold-blooded act."

"Does anyone else know about what you found Ciara?"

"No, only you. I didn't want to go forward with it unless you felt it had some merit. I don't know what the Sheriff's forensics department has yet either; they're going over my autopsy findings as we speak."

"Thank you Ciara. Be careful not to discuss this with anyone, as we don't yet know whose involved with these killings. If anyone in law enforcement asks you about these cases, show them where the files are and let them find what they can. And let me know immediately if that should happen, would you?"

"It sounds like you have a hunch or two already; do you?" Ciara asked.

"Just something in my gut; nothing specific at this time. Maybe after I go over your notes and talk to the sheriff. I'll keep you in the loop. Let's get out of here. How about stopping at Sam's for a night cap. Are you up for one tonight?"

"How about a rain check; give me a call this week?"

"Sure. Be careful, and don't tell any more of those Irish jokes, will you?" Matt kidded as he and Ciara headed for their cars.

He walked her to where she was parked, turned towards her as they arrived at her car and slipped his arms around her, pressing himself against her. "I hope you don't give up on me."

"Not a chance."

And with that their lips moved towards each others, both of them feeling each other's anxiety as they stood there kissing.

That night after he got back to his apartment Matt poured over Ciara's notes. One thing for sure, based on her information and his instincts, almost assuredly all twelve murders had been committed by one killer; one left handed serial killer who was still out there somewhere, possibly planning or even committing the next murder. Matt had to decide if he should share the newfound information with the sheriff, or wait until he was fully grounded in the case. He was concerned that if the press were to get a hold of the information there would be wide-spread panic throughout the County. And that it may even drive the killer under ground, or possibly away from the area completely.

No matter what was done at this point, it would not dismiss or alter the fact that Maricopa County, and all cities within its boundary, had a serial killer bent on claiming a victim every week, until caught! Men, women, and even children were not safe.

CHAPTER 3

The first thing Matt did in the morning was to meet with Sheriff Haynes. The sheriff clued him into what was going on, explaining that with twelve current homicides his office needed expert investigative help. He did not indicate to Matt that they were looking at the cases as serial murders. In fact, no mention was made of it. Matt told the sheriff he'd be willing to help and asked the sheriff to have his office manager call the various departments he would need access to and let them know that full cooperation was to be granted. The sheriff introduced Matt to the lead officer in charge of the cases and then left him to fend for himself, asking him to provide a status report weekly.

The next few days were busy for Matt. He visited the last three crime scenes and compared the data in the sheriff's files to his own observations. This made him realize immediately how 'limited' the sheriff's office was in the area of investigative protocols and forensic evidence gathering.

Matt poured over his notes, reading them out loud to himself:

'Victim twelve; Harold Cummings, retired accountant living in Sun City. Throat cut starting from just below the right ear, through the carotid artery, ending just under the left jaw line. Either as an afterthought or to assure a successful kill, he was then stabbed in the heart, severing the right aorta. Victim found sitting in his easy chair, with a book lying on the floor next to his feet. In the book an envelope was found; the contents of which was not in the police report; a parking ticket?

'Found small black particle of something lying partially hidden between the cushion of the victim's chair and the inside of the chair -- leather, plastic, rubber? Have it checked. No indication of break in; victim must have let the killer in and then felt comfortable enough to sit down in easy chair afterwards. All valuables still intact; robbery is not indicated as a motive.

'Victim eleven; John Willette; 36 year old bachelor living in a small rental home in the city of Glendale; approximately six miles from victim twelve. Found in living room, lying face down with single 9mm GSW to the back of the head. Police report indicated the victim's television was still on but the sound was muted. Blood splatter indicated he was walking towards the kitchen when shot from behind. Bullet went through skull and lodged in a kitchen cabinet, just below the sink. Trajectory of bullet indicates the killer was taller than victim, shot at a downward angle. Victim still had wallet, watch, and rings on his person; robbery not the motive.

'Victim ten; Valerie Encinitas, 49, divorced. Lived at mother's home in Mesa, approximately 39 miles from victim eleven and 45 miles from victim twelve. Victim was found in her car, in the parking lot of a Fry's super market with multiple stab wounds, one of which entered her heart, and another her left carotid artery. A few more entered her abdomen and chest. Again, purse and all possessions were still in the car; the motor was still running when she was found. Her window was down, and the wounds indicated she was stabbed through the driver side window. No defensive cuts were inflicted to her hands or arms. Surveillance cameras did not cover the portion of the lot where her car was parked. Review of the camera footage at the approximate time of attack showed a number of pedestrian cars entering and leaving that specific area, as well as a security truck which found the victim, a police car and a couple of service vehicles; not sure if local or not.'

Matt spent the remainder of the fourth day on the case reviewing the coroner's files, sheriff's files and local police files, along with his own notes. He had come to the conclusion that the killer was not part of the general public, but someone who worked for a provider of services such as power, water, gardening, plumbing, electrical, etc., or, some governmental service, or agency. Robbery was definitely not the motive; the killer was left handed, and had access to at least three guns and one knife. In Arizona, that could mean just about anyone!

"Ciara, I need your help; could I drop by your office for a few minutes?"

"Of course you can drop by. I've missed you. What do you have, anything?"

"Possibly. I found something at one of the crime scenes and I don't want to go thru the sheriff's office to find out what it is; can you take a look at it with your microscope? Probably nothing," Matt said, "but then again, who knows."

He drove over to where Ciara worked and gave her the envelope containing the little black piece of material. "This is it. Could you examine it and let me know what it is; give me a call when you get done?"

"Will do. Find out anything else yet, looking a those crime scenes?"

"I have a few notes of things I'm going to follow up on; probably nothing significant but you know the old saying – leave no rock unturned."

"What does the sheriff's team think about what you've found?"

"They don't know anything yet; disclosure at this time is not warranted. And you be sure you keep this under your cap for now. I don't want them getting up in arms about me calling on you for forensic help, when they have a whole forensic department over there. Ok?"

"It's going to cost you!" Ciara said, with that impish smile of hers.

"I'll write out a check right now; how much?"

"It's not money you'll be payin' laddie. I'm keepin' a talley and your day of reckoning will come!"

"I can't wait. I need to leave now though Ciara; see you later." And with that he left for his office and further planning. He needed to report his first weeks work to the sheriff in a couple of days and full disclosure was not an option; at least not just yet.

CHAPTER 4

Jason Little worked as a field rep for a local cable company. He had a friendly disposition for the most part, and liked talking with people. He drove all over the 'Valley of the Sun' visiting customers who needed his services for one reason or another. His office was located in the city of Peoria, bordering Sun City and the city of El Mora. His home was in the city of Surprise; not more than a 12 mile one way trip to the office. The only thing he hated about the trip was that the quickest way to get from his home to work was to go down US-60, which ran through the city limits of El Mora; at that point it's called Grand Avenue. Of course, anyone who had lived in Arizona for the past five years knew about the 'Photo Radar' wars and how the State, and a lot of cities, had installed photo radar traps thinking they would be a huge source of revenue under the guise of making it safer for the public. Jason was always getting his picture taken by the city of El Mora's 'US-60' trap, either while driving to work in his own car or while driving his company truck. Of course, he never received a notice when he was in the company truck because the law excluded corporations from being cited. But when he was in his own car, sure enough within two weeks of the strobe light going off, he would get a notice indicating he had been caught speeding, or going through the red light where the radar had been set up.

It was Tuesday afternoon when Jason arrived home, picked up his mail and found a notice from El Mora indicating their photo radar camera had caught him while in his personal car. He opened it, read it, ripped it up and threw it in the trash just like the previous three he had received from them. Since he lived in a guarded and gated community it was difficult for the process servers to make contact with him at home. And since they worked at nights, and on weekends, that is where he stayed; behind a locked gate that lead into his courtyard and to his front door. On one occasion he was served and summoned to court after he hadn't sent in a check. But since he had made it a habit, after his first notice, to always drive down Grand Avenue while in his own car with the sun visor down shielding his face, the pictures didn't conclusively show it was him driving, and the court dismissed the citation. He had also covered his personal license plate with a plastic see-thru shield. It was spray painted with clear enamel creating a glare when the camera went off, making it difficult to see the plate number, thus no notice could be sent. He felt pretty good considering he knew for sure the camera had gone off over thirteen times while in his personal car, and only four notices had arrived; this one being the fourth. He didn't consider himself a criminal for his actions as he felt the traps were unfair, with the signal lights set up to intentionally make it difficult to stop in a safe manner. Little did Mr. Little know that his actions did not go un-noticed. Since the City of El Mora's administrative offices were located directly across from their Grand Avenue radar trap, a police car was always parked there, and someone on the force was usually in it watching and waiting, and number thirteen for Jason would end up being his unlucky number.

A month had gone by since Jason had torn up his last photo radar notice and he felt pretty safe now. No process servers had been reported by the security guard company, hired by his HOA. It was Friday and he felt like a few drinks after dinner would be a good way to come down from the work week. Maybe dinner at Applebee's with a few drinks at the bar. It was only a mile from his house; a few hundred steps from the walk-thru security gate. So he had decided to walk over; the November night being cool and he needed the exercise. He ordered their savory fire-grilled cedar salmon with a medley of vegetables and steamed potatoes. And instead of drinks at the bar, Jason paired the grilled salmon with a V. Sattui Gamay Rouge 2012 rose' wine; what a way to end a night he thought as he left the restaurant for his walk back home.

The security gate at the back of Jason's complex was not manned, just gated. It looked a long ways off as he began walking down the narrow winding road leading towards it. The night was dark now and chillier since he had first started out a few hours previous, so he zipped up his blue windbreaker and put his hands in the pockets. He thought how much he loved the smell of the wet grass, and the trees that lined the road, and the wispy sounds they made as the breezes traveled through them. In a split second he felt a tug on his neck and then everything seemed strange. It was as though he was staring up at the clear night sky, with all of its stars twinkling down at him. And then Jason had no more thoughts, as the last drop of his life gushed its crimson stream onto the grass, whose smell was no more.

CHAPTER 5

Matt was about to go downtown to meet with the sheriff, and the police chiefs who were involved with the investigation, when his phone rang.

"Matt, Ciara. Got another one on the table; just came in this morning. Looks like the same MO; neck slit from victim's right side to left. No other wounds this time though. They found him just outside a gated community – cops said he lived there."

"No good morning or how's the whether or something; just stab 'em and slab 'em? Does it look like the same kind of knife was used?"

"Well, good morning. And yes, it looks like the same type of knife blade made the cut. Do you want to come down and take a look?"

"I'm about to go meet with the sheriff and the chief's of police; I'll come by afterwards. See you then."

Sheriff Haynes was a man of few words, unless he was in front of reporters or a camera. When Matt gave him his report for the week the sheriff said he thought it would be best to meet with the chief of police of each city where a murder had been committed. Matt agreed but asked the sheriff to try and see if he could create an atmosphere that forced each chief to discuss their thoughts on the cases. He wanted to see what their attitudes were relative to the approach they were taking.

"Good morning gentlemen," the sheriff began. "I want to introduce you to Matt Bower, retired Captain of the homicide division of Washington, DC. He currently has his own private investigation business here in Phoenix. A couple of you have worked with him before. I've asked Matt to help investigate these recent murders in order to get a fresh perspective, which will hopefully help each of our jurisdictions. My intent for calling this meeting, however, was not just to introduce Matt, but to have us disclose and discuss what each has found out up to this point in time. My IT specialist, Ray Overton here, will also be working with me to gather and analyze the data we come up with over the course of the investigation. Since I provided each of you in advance with an agenda of the meeting, let's begin; Chief Watson from Mesa, where is your department relative to the case involving the one murder over there."

One by one, each of the Chiefs went through the cases involving the victims in their jurisdictions, as Mr. Overton input their information into his laptop's database. There was only one chief left when they were about to break for lunch; Chief James Arbaugh from El Mora.

"Look sheriff, I thought we would be done by lunch so I scheduled other things for this afternoon; we'll have to do this some other time," Arbaugh stated rather emphatically.

"Jim, that's why I sent each of you the agenda showing how much time we would be spending here. If it's all right with everyone, let's skip the lunch break so Jim can provide his input. Jim, you're up."

"Sorry everyone, but I have more important matters to contend with. We'll have to make it some other time", and with that Chief Arbaugh got up to leave the room.

"Chief Arbaugh, just a second, let me walk out with you," Matt said as he got up and followed the Chief out of the room. He pulled a pen from his shirt pocket and grabbed a piece of paper from the table as he went out the door to catch up with the chief.

"These meetings can sometimes bite into your day can't they?" Matt said to the chief as he moved around in front of him. He stood in the chief's path of retreat and handed the pen and paper to him, explaining "Could you write down your cell phone number for me in case I come up with anything of importance to share with you?"

The chief took the pen and paper from him, wrote down his number, handed it back and without saying another word walked away.

"Thanks", Matt said as he stood there watching Chief Arbaugh leave the building. Without looking at the number that the chief had scribbled, he placed the paper and pen in his pocket and returned to the meeting room, just in time to say good-by to the others. Sheriff Haynes and his IT guy were just standing up from the table when Matt entered and sat down in the chair next to the sheriff; the sheriff and Ray Overton sat back down.

"So, what do you think about what we heard today? Any new pieces to help put the puzzle together?", the sheriff asked Matt.

"Yes and no. More no, however, than yes. How long have you known Chief Arbaugh sheriff?"

"Well, he was hired by the city of El Mora five years ago. I've never really made it a point to interact with him on a personal basis but we've known each other most of that time on a professional level. Why?"

"Didn't you think it was rather strange how he intentionally set other appointments that would take him away from this meeting, after he had heard from all the other chiefs? I mean, if someone sent me an agenda of a meeting I was going to attend and participate in at a specific time, but knew in advance that I wouldn't be able to participate at that time, wouldn't it be appropriate to call and ask to have the agenda changed so you could participate, or at least call and excuse yourself?"

"I got the distinct impression of unprofessionalism on his part, especially since he called and asked to go last" the sheriff said. "He's always been an odd fellow though, so I just chalked it up to that. Considering that five of the murdered victims were in his jurisdiction he should have felt and obligation to share what he and his department have found out so far. I hope he isn't hiding the fact that he just doesn't have anything to disclose at this time. Although I wouldn't be surprised if that were the case; this whole thing is turning out to be like trying to grab a slippery eel. He shouldn't have taken that attitude though."

"Well, I'm going back to my office and go over all of the info we heard this morning and see if anything pops out at me. I'll talk to you later sheriff." Matt turned towards Ray Overton, "good to have met you Ray."

"Matt, how can you remember everything that was said in the meeting? I'm sure Ray had a hard enough time keeping up himself, and he's fast."

Matt pulled a pen from his pocket and handed it to the sheriff: "Push up on the clip of the pen sheriff." When he did, a recording of the meeting started to play. He then took the pen back, and with that he left Sheriff Haynes with his mouth half open. He returned to his office after he stopped by to see Ciara and go over the most current victim's findings with her. Jason Little's murder had definitely been committed by the same left handed killer and the knife had left the same marks.

Matt had found out some very interesting facts about the crime scenes that the other chief's had investigated. All of them, with the exception of the child, had been visibly aware of their killer. None of them seem to have been surprised or overpowered in advance of their demise. This substantiated his findings relative to the three scenes he had investigated. Also, two of the chief's had substantiated that the same kind of knife blade was used. It was partially serrated and a small puncture of the skin was evident next to those wounds where the knife had been plunged into the victim. Dr. Caddell had also mentioned something about a mark the killer's knife had left. He knew at that point in time the cases were all tied together and he was sure it would lead to a single murderer; a serial killer with an attitude.

CHAPTER 6

When Matt got back to his office Marcy had a surprise for him. Sitting on his desk was a brand new laptop computer! His old one had died a week ago and he had been going crazy not being able to read his emails or do any investigative work surfing the web.

"Hey Marcy, is our hot spot still up and running; can I get this new laptop to connect to the web?"

"What do you think I am, just a beautiful face and body? It's already connected and I set up a password for you to access it with. Is it worth a free lunch?"

"Well, let's put it this way. Unless I have that password in front of me in the next five seconds, you may be working thru dinner if you know what I mean!"

"Look in the top drawer of your desk grumpy, then swallow the piece of paper it's written on, and I hope you choke!"

Matt took out the piece of paper with the password inscribed on it and laughed as he booted the laptop up to the password screen. He typed in the password 'im1jackass', hit the enter key and voila! He was staring at a whole new world called 'Apple'.

"Thank you Marcy. Every time I come to work and see you sitting there I'll remember my password; very ingenious!"

Marcy yelled out, "Looser", and then kicked the door shut between their work spaces.

The next hour or so Matt worked on getting use to the new technology. Using his finger as a mouse was very intuitive. He learned to 'hover' the mouse pointer over the icon called 'Safari' then tap his finger to 'click' and all of a sudden he was able to surf the web!

"I need to isolate the type of knife that is being used," he mumbled to himself. After a little while of surfing the web, he picked up the phone and called Ciara's cell.

"What's been happening," Ciara said as she recognized who the call was from.

"Well, I need your expert input. A couple of the police chiefs also felt that one specific knife is being used and I'm trying to find it on the web. They said something similar to you, in that the knife left a 'puncture' mark around the major wounds. You said you thought the hilt may have left marks. Do you feel the marks were 'punctures' or hilt bruises? And could you tell how long of a blade the knife was?"

"I think you could classify the bruises as punctures, approximately one eighth inch in diameter. And the blade length is approximately four inches. Why, have you found a knife that may fit the bill?"

"I'm looking now; sending you a link to a site that shows a knife that may be the one. The only thing is though, the blade is partly serrated and you made no mention of that in the report."

"I'm just clicking on the link you sent and it's coming up now. Let's see, a 'SOG Pentagon Elite 1'.

Yes, that potentially could be the blade and I see that it has a locking mechanism that, when open, a metal clasp protrudes out. Yes, yes, that could definitely be the blade. The serrations are very small and only about 1" in length. The blade is four inches and when unfolded the length is 8.75". Definitely long enough to get a good grip on and yet small enough, when folded, to conceal. Let me get one and I'll have forensics test it."

"Excellent. And don't tell anyone about the results or the tests. Let forensics know this is not to be disclosed to anyone! Call me when you get the results. Thanks Ciara."

Matt needed to get away from the work for a while and one of his most favorite diversion activities was to go to a shooting range, just outside of town on the Pleasant View Highway. So he packed up part of his 'arsenal' and headed for the range. He only took four of his rifles and three of his handguns, along with enough ammo to start a war! He got settled in at one of the shooting stations; guns laid out with clips and boxes of ammo conveniently placed. He was sitting there with one of his paper targets in his lap when the signal went off indicating all shooters could safely place their targets on the range. He got up and proceeded to walk out on the range to position his target. Since he would be starting his practice with a 45 millimeter Glock, he placed the target ten yards out. As he was returning to his station he looked left for a second and got a glimpse of a shooter a number of stations down from his that had a familiar gait. Matt had developed an acute sense of presence and sharp memory of people's movements. He didn't think much of it at the time and concentrated on his shooting.

After about an hour or so, Matt decided to get a cold can of soda from the range's snack and ammo shop. As he was walking past the other shooting stations he looked beyond the ammo shop to a station at the far end of the range and saw a familiar face; it was Chief Arbaugh from the city of El Mora! From his vantage point he could see that the chief was also a collector of guns, and that he was dressed in 'camo' gear from head to boots; hardly recognizable unless you had sat directly across from the man for three hours in a meeting the previous day. Matt decided to pay him a visit, as distasteful as the thought was. So he walked down to the chief's shooting station.

"Chief Arbaugh. Looks like we have a mutual interest in guns," Matt said in a friendly tone.

The chief looked up at him with a surprised look that immediately turned dirt cold. "I don't think we have any mutual interests Mr. Bower."

"Possibly not; you may be right. Especially considering the ignorant way you conducted yourself at the meeting yesterday. Seems like you intentionally attended the meeting to obtain as much information as possible, without disclosing anything yourself."

Chief Arbaugh was a lean 195 lb, 6' 3" man who could be intimidating if you weren't an ex-marine/ex-homicide captain. He stopped what he was doing, slowly pushed himself up from his shooting station, moved one step towards Matt, stood a few inches from his face and stared him in the eyes. "I don't like you Mr. Bower. I would be careful if I was you to not overstep your bounds and think you have any jurisdiction, or authority, in the investigations you participate in. And I would especially caution you not to find yourself in my jurisdiction with the hint of alcohol on your breath, you drunken ex-cop!"

For the first time in years Matt was staring at what he referred to as 'dead eyes'; eyes disclosing that the brain behind them had no compunction when it came to killing. His hunch about the type of person Arbaugh was seemed to be panning out correctly. His words to Arbaugh brought out just what he thought they would; a person not fit to wear the uniform of a peace officer. It was also interesting to know that Arbaugh had taken the time to look into Matt's personal life, knowing about his issue with alcohol.

"Thanks for the warning, I'll take it into consideration", and with that Matt walked back to the ammo shop, got his drink and returned to his shooting station. He finished for the day, all the while thinking about how he was going to handle Chief Arbaugh. Should he tell the sheriff about his encounter with Arbaugh? Probably not at this time. He would have to see how things played out from this point on. One thing he did find out from his encounter with Arbaugh; the man had a number of hand guns. The ones he saw included a 22 millimeter, and two 9 millimeter. He also noticed Arbaugh had a small sheath protruding from his side pocket; one just the size to carry a folding four inch knife that could be easily accessed by a left handed person. And Arbaugh's shooting station was set up to accommodate a left-handed person. But Arbaugh used his right hand when he asked him to pen down his phone number at the meeting the other day. Were Matt's suspicions about Arbaugh proving to be correct? Right then he could only think of one thing he needed badly and it wasn't the soda he was drinking. Possibly a visit to an El Mora bar might be in Matt's future?

CHAPTER 7

Matt's office was located on the second floor of an old building on Central Avenue in downtown Phoenix. As he came down the hallway and approached his office he looked at the poorly painted signage located on the glass portion of the entry door: 'Matt Bower – Prive Investigator' and thought to himself what an idiot he had been to pick someone off the street to do the work. He reminded himself, as he had done a hundred times before, to get at least the 'Prive' portion removed so potential clients didn't think he investigated toilets! He would ask Marcy, again, to take care of it.

He opened the door, "Hey Marcy, either scrape that 'Prive' off with a razor blade or get someone up here to fix it, unless you actually want to start investigating toilets!"

Marcy's body jumped two inches out of her chair, surprised by Matt's quiet approach to the office. Usually she could hear him coming in sufficient time to prepare herself if she needed to, for some unknown clandestine reason. "Jeez boss, don't surprise me that way. I almost had a coronary."

He looked over her shoulder at her computer monitor and saw a screen full of hyper babble; he couldn't make any sense of it. "What's that?" he asked.

"It's programming code. I'm working on hacking into the justice system's database. Thought it might help us in our investigations. In fact, I just ran across a back door to all traffic violations filed throughout the state. Want to find out who has pending citations?"

"Can anyone trace this back to us?" he asked with a worried look on his face.

"Of course not. I'm routing all of our activity through five different Servers worldwide using encrypted terminal and router id numbers that change every three minutes. There is no way in hell someone could trace it back to here. Unless, of course, they wrote a specific program to do so and then they would have to know what server is the host. And I've written a program that changes our server's id number every three minutes as well. So it would take a room full of high powered servers running a highly sophisticated set of programs to find us. Feel better?"

"No, but I'll take your word for it. Get that 'Prive' removed from our door would you please, for the umpteenth time?" and he started for his office when he stopped abruptly. "You said you could find out who has traffic citations? Do me a favor. Run a list of all the victim's names through that database and let me know what comes up will you? It would be interesting to see if any of them pop up, and in what municipality."

"Will do boss. What do you want first, the 'Prive' or the data?" she said with a big smile on her face.

"I want them both! Now!" and he went into his office, shut the door and began talking to himself. "Need to give her a raise or she'll be out of here soon. She's too valuable to loose. And it's hard to find someone who can put up with me."

Over the remainder of the day Matt spent surfing the web, trying to find some background info on Arbaugh. He ran a credit report and found out the guy was squeaky clean on that side of the equation. A confidential background investigation report showed he had been employed by some backwater town as a police officer for two years prior to his employment with the city of El Mora. He was initially hired as assistant chief but after a year, when the chief had a bout of food poisoning that lasted a couple of weeks, Arbaugh took over as acting chief. The old chief never really recovered and the city ended up replacing him with Arbaugh. Matt sent an inquiry letter to his previous employer requesting the circumstances under which Arbaugh left their employment; all he could do now was wait for their response.

Maybe he was looking in the wrong direction. Maybe Arbaugh was in his sights because of a personality difference or something else he couldn't put his finger on. He decided to leave it that way for the time being. His apartment was a refuge to him, so he called it a day knowing tomorrow would bring the same challenges. Hopefully the murderer would wait the allotted time between his kills and the county wouldn't start the next day with another victim.

Even as he was thinking these thoughts a trucker named Mike Wharton turned his Kenworth's right directional signal on to exit the freeway.

Two more blocks and he was in the process of parking his big rig in the open field next to a tract of houses where he lived. As he did so, he saw a red light in his rear view mirror. He set the parking break, shifted into park, turned the key off and sat in the cab, waiting for the cop to approach the truck. After a couple of minutes and no cop he decided he should get out and see what was going on. He opened the door of the cab, and with some effort slid his large belly past the steering wheel, stepped down onto the running board and turned his face towards the cab before stepping down onto the ground. As his foot touched the ground his left hand slammed the door closed while his body swiveled around to face the back of the truck.

Shock flooded over his whole body as he found himself face to face with a police officer. His eyes locked onto the cop's eyes and a cold shiver ran down his neck and back; those eyes looked almost dead he thought. He took a step backwards, hoping it would place him in a comfort zone he always liked to find when confronting the law.

"Whoa, you scared the living daylights out of me officer, what seems to be the problem?" Mike asked.

"You made an illegal signal back there; license and registration please."

"What do you mean? I put my directional signal on more than 300 feet from the off ramp; more than the law requires."

"You put your left signal on to make a right turn, now let me see your license and registration."

Mike again felt a chill run down his back. This cop was giving off some real bad vibes. He knew for sure he hadn't put the wrong directional signal on but he just wanted to get this over with and get into his house so he could take a nice warm shower and relax from his long trip. So he turned to get back up into his cab where the truck's registration papers were kept. He opened the door, stepped up on the running board and as he looked up into the cab he saw the inside of his windshield all of a sudden turn red; his last thought was 'how did that happen', then his lifeless body was thrown forward onto the seat of the cab, no more to feel the warmth of a shower.

****

Matt arrived at his office the next day before Marcy so he booted up his laptop and opened one of the files he had been working on prior to getting involved with the county murders. After all, he still needed to work on finishing up his existing commitments. Just as he finished writing up a few notes in the file, Marcy arrived and burst into his office.

"Hey boss, do I have a wad load of good news for you! I almost called you last night but got so involved with my daughter's homework, then my coding a program, it was too late."

"Is it a good wad or bad wad of info?" Matt said as he sat back and took in the sight of Marcy. She looked like she had transformed into a computer programmer or something like it. She was wearing pants, a pair of loafers, white blouse and a tight button down pin-striped vest; all of varying colors and styles! "You look like your closet exploded all over you; what's going on?"

"Yes, well let me tell you the news first. Yesterday I worked on that list of victims and tapping into the state's database of traffic citations to see if any of them had citations, and guess what?"

"Your program blew up? I don't know, what."

"Every name I entered had at least four hits, or citations; some had over ten over the past two years! Now what are the odds of that happening?" She said as she put both her hands flat on his desk and leaned towards his face with big eyes staring at him.

Matt sat there stupefied. He didn't know if it was because of her findings, or because of Marcy herself. He stared back at her for a full five seconds not saying a thing.

"Every one of them has had multiple traffic citations? In the past 24 months? Are you sure your program didn't go haywire or something; garbage in garbage out? That's pretty hard to imagine if you think about it for a minute," he questioned.

"My program did just what it was supposed to. In fact, if you think about it without considering these people as victims but just a set of drivers who reside in a database of thousands of names and you asked it to give you those who had more than four citations in the last two years, then its just a list of such drivers. In fact, once I ran their names individually against the database and got a hit on everyone of them, I decided to write a query that gave me a list of every driver who met those same parameters, and guess what?"

"You got the same list of names?" Matt responded.

"Yes, and no."

"What do you mean, yes and no? It's either or; can't be both!"

"Well smarty, it is both. The new list has every one of their names, plus nine more! A sum total of twenty-two!" Marcy finished with a look on her face like a cat that had just swallowed the mouse; very satisfied.

Matt's mind was reeling. Had she found the link that bound the victims together? But something was gnawing at him. The list was not only of those who had been killed, but also of nine others who hadn't. What did that mean? Or what didn't it mean?

"Marcy, you're supreme! How much do I pay you an hour?"

"Not enough, I would say!" Marcy replied, with a grin on her face.

"Well, starting immediately I'm increasing your pay by fifty percent; no, make that twenty-five percent. And you're worth every penny of it. Now get out of here and let me cogitate the 'wad' of info you've given me. Leave me a list of the twenty-two names and save a copy to the file. And by the way, I noticed by the sign on our door that we no longer investigate 'Prives'; thanks for following through Marcy. And I like your outfit."

She went back to her desk, propped her feet up on the desktop, crossed her legs, leaned back in her chair and thought 'wow Marcy, I guess you can now get that apartment and buy some new clothes for Cindy; maybe Matt is the real thing'. She also wondered if she should have told him about how Ray, the sheriff's IT guy, helped her out. And then the phone rang, interrupting her train of thought. It was Ciara from the morgue. Not good news.

CHAPTER 8

"Hey Matt. Sorry it's me that always calls to give you bad news, but another body was added last night. Looks like the guy was killed over thirty-six hours ago. His wife called it in when she saw his truck parked outside in the field next to their home. He was lying on the front seat of the cab of his truck; a bullet in the back of the head. I haven't done an autopsy yet but when I finish I'll give you a call."

"That's definitely not good news. Especially if it's related to the other killings as it's only been four days since the last one. The killer may be moving his schedule up for some reason. Hope it's not because he's getting jittery due to the investigation. By the way, was the victim's name any of the following?" He began reading off the nine names from the list Marcy gave him and when he said 'Mike Wharton' Ciara yelled out.

"That's him! Mike Wharton is the victim's name! Where did you, how did you get his name?" Ciara asked excitedly.

Matt took the time to explain the whole thing to her and how all the others who had been killed were on the list. He also told her that there were eight more names who could become potential future victims.

"What are you going to do about the others Matt? How are you going to assure they don't become victims?"

"I think its time to let the sheriff in on what we've found and ask for his help. This is just too much for one person. I also need to tell him about my hunch regarding Arbaugh. Maybe we can work this from two different angles so that no one else is killed. Ciara, make sure you're aware of your surroundings will you, and don't take any chances? Always be with someone, and when you travel, check around you, in your back seat, etc. I'm not saying this to frighten you but to make sure you know how dangerous this guy is to all involved in this investigation. Ok?"

"Will do. Remember, I carry and can shoot. You didn't waste all of your time on the range with me. I'm pretty good you know."

"I know, but it's usually when you least expect it that you-know-what hits the fan. And you may not get a chance to practice your shooting; remember that will you? I'll call you later, after I talk to the sheriff." Matt said this in a kind and caring tone, then hung up and called the sheriff to set up a meeting with him.

"Sheriff Haynes, thanks for meeting with me on such short notice. I think its time for me to come clean with what I've found out so far, that you don't already know. I need your help if we're going to stop these killings."

"That's why I hired you Matt. What have you found out?"

Matt brought the sheriff up to speed on all of his findings including his hunches about Chief Arbaugh. They then focused on how they were going to assure the other eight people who were on the 'victims' list stayed alive. The sheriff said he would select a trustworthy group of sheriff's posse members who were not 'paid officers', who were dedicated to the sheriff's office and assign them to watch over the eight 'potential victims'. He would also immediately assign a group to 'inconspicuously' watch Chief Arbaugh on a 24/7 basis, with instructions to call Matt directly if anything looked suspicious or if the two group's paths crossed in any way. Matt's number was put on the sheriff's personal phones' speed dial so he could be notified at a moments notice.

"Ok sheriff, I think we have all bases covered. If my hunch is right, and the killer is moving his schedule up, we shouldn't have to wait too long. Let's see how things go from here," and with that he left the sheriff to carry out the work ahead.

Marcy had been at work for about six hours when the phone rang; Matt was on the other end. He hadn't checked in all day so she was relieved to hear his voice.

"Hey there, how are things going around the office; any messages for me?"

"Ciara called and said for you to call her when you get a chance. The sheriff sent over a sealed envelope for you; hopefully it's not a bomb! Chief Arbaugh called fifteen minutes ago to see if you were in and wanted to know when you would return. And..." Marcy was stopped in midsentence by Matt.

"What did you tell Chief Arbaugh Marcy?"

"That you weren't in and I didn't expect you to come in; that's all. Why?"

"Marcy, listen to me and do exactly what I tell you; don't ask questions. Reach over and lock the door - now; do it."

"Ok, done, now what?" Marcy said with apprehension and a little fear in her voice.

"Hang up, go into my room and lock the door behind you. Then go to my desk and in the lower right hand drawer there's a gun; get it and sit against the wall that's solid concrete, with the back of my chair facing the outside window. The chair's back has a two inch thick piece of steel in it for protection; keep your head below the top of the chair. When I hang up I'll be coming there directly from where I am. It'll take about fifteen minutes though. If you hear someone trying to get in, tell them to identify themselves and to wait outside in the hallway. Tell them there's a bomb inside and help is on the way. If anyone tries to break into the office, turn the chair around for protection and be prepared to shoot them, especially if they identify themselves as a 'Chief Arbaugh', do you understand Marcy?"

"I think so Matt. Should I hang up now?

"Yes, and remember, I'm on my way. There should not be any city police coming to help; only myself. Got it? Be prepared to shoot anyone else, remembering the laws relative to concealed weapons I taught you!"

"Hurry Matt, I'm scared. Hurry," and with that she hung up and immediately did what he had instructed her.

Time passed for Marcy as if the clock was standing still. She felt perspiration running down her right temple as she sat in Matt's chair, the 9 millimeter Glock in her right hand pointed towards the door, her left hand cradling it for support. She knew Glocks didn't have a safety so she had pulled the slide of the receiver back to place a bullet in the chamber and lowered the hammer gently, finger off the trigger, ready to fire. Thoughts of her daughter came into her mind. What would Cindy do without her? Her mother would take good care of her. Would anyone else care? How about Matt? She couldn't let him down, with all the work he had. She liked her job, and many other mindless things popped into her head. All of a sudden, the outside door was being shaken and the sound reverberated throughout the office.

"Marcy, its me, are you alright? Unbolt the door and let me in."

Marcy rushed to the first door and unlocked it, then ran to the outside door and was about to unbolt it when a horrible thought rushed through her mind; what if it's not Matt? She could see the silhouette of a man standing on the other side of the door and she immediately moved to the side so she wasn't in front of the glass portion of it and pointed the gun at the figure.

"Matt, if it's you, what's your laptop's password?"

A few seconds of silence followed, then "im1jackass".

Marcy quickly unlocked the door, threw it open and jumped into Matt's arms!

He wrapped his arms around her and waited a few moments for things to calm down, then without missing a beat he said, "Wow, I guess that raise was too much if this is the greeting I get when I come to work!"

Marcy, still in Matt's arms, looked into his eyes and gave him a passionate kiss. Then she slowly let go of him and said, "Aren't you glad you saved me? There's always more where that came from."

Matt looked down at Marcy's hand that held the gun, took it from her and said, "Is everything alright here now?", ignoring her overt comment.

"I think so. Clue me in on why you scared the living crap out of me?"

"Just a precaution; I probably overreacted but I thought it best to error on the side of caution. Any more calls from Chief Arbaugh?"

"No. But just after you hung up a man from a company named SafePhoto-RD called wanting to talk to you. I have his number if you need it. His name is Don Soliari"

"SafePhoto-RD? The name sounds familiar but I can't remember where I've heard it. I'll Google it. Now, let's get back to work. Sorry I frightened you Marcy. In the future never tell anyone where I am. Just tell them you expect me back any moment and take a message, got it?"

"Got it boss. And just forget that thing I did when you came through the door ok? It won't happen again," Marcy said with an inquisitive sound in her voice as she turned and went back to her desk.

CHAPTER 9

Matt knew he had heard 'SafePhoto-RD' before and started to talk to himself as he began his research. 'I know I've heard that name before. Let's see what Google's got on SafePhoto-RD. Ok...SafePhoto-RD, a traffic safety company that provides photo radar and surveillance services world wide. A multi-billion dollar industry. Wikipedia indicates photo radar cameras have what is called 'automatic plate recognition' that can be used by governments for mass surveillance, as needed. It looks like, from all these posts, photo radar cameras are a big issue here in the U.S., and in Europe. In fact, here are a number of posts that indicate insiders of SafePhoto-RD are being investigated for illegal payoffs to federal, state and local politicians to assure any negative legislation doesn't get passed. One judge, who ordered them illegal in his jurisdiction and required the county to refund drivers, mysteriously went missing and has not been located to this day. Looks like I need to meet with 'SafePhoto-RD' tomorrow and see why they're barking up my tree.'

Matt looked up SafePhoto-RD's local address on the web, grabbed the business card of Don Soliari, verified that it was the same address and told Marcy he was leaving for the day, and for her to take the rest of the day off. He then drove to SafePhoto-RD's facilities located outside the town of Tolleson; about a forty minute trip from downtown Phoenix. The thought of calling in advance crossed his mind but he needed to get out of the office and a surprise visit might reveal more than a planned one.

He drove around their facilities, which covered about 25 fully fenced acres, to get a feel for the operation and a lay of the land. There was a guard shack at the entry, which seemed strange to him for some reason. He handed the guard Mr. Soliari's card, introduced himself and said he was there to see Soliari. After a couple of minutes, and a phone call, the guard activated the security gate and directed him to proceed to building 'B' where Mr. Soliari would be waiting for him. He entered building 'B' and was greeted by a well-dressed receptionist who, after saying a few sentences, he knew was definitely not there because of her intellectual prowess. She motioned him to proceed through a door, which she buzzed to open.

As the door closed, Matt found himself staring down a long sterile looking hallway with a number of doors on the left side. About thirty feet down the hall a man in a business suite appeared from one of the office doors and started walking towards him. The man was athletic looking, shorter than himself, dark complexion, black hair and a chiseled look to his face. Matt didn't see any sign of friendliness in the man's face; no creases at the eyes or lips to indicate a jovial temperament, or even a hint of being able to smile. Not even a wrinkle on his forehead; someone not prone to fear or worry.

"Mr. Bower? My name is Don Soliari, welcome to SafePhoto-RD." Soliari extended his arm to shake Matt's hand.

Matt felt the steel hard hand of a professional as he shook Soliari's hand. It was definitely not a hand of someone who sat behind a desk all day or pushed a pencil. He had felt that toughness before and his guard went up.

"If you'll follow me we'll go into the conference room just past my office. Did you have any problem finding the place? Our location is a bit off the beaten path."

"No problem at all. Quite a large parcel of land you have here. You must have some valuable equipment or assets, to warrant a guard shack and double hung razor wire on your fences. Many attempted break-ins?"

Soliari took a moment to scrutinize the man who stood before him; his build, the cut of his clothes, the eyes and how he postured himself and his body. In a moment of thought he knew, this man was going to be a formidable foe. "No more than normal. We have a significant amount of trucks and equipment that is specialized in nature so security is imperative. Won't you have a seat?" Soliari motioned him to sit down in one of the chairs around a conference table as he moved to the head of it.

Matt declined the suggested seat and walked to another chair which was positioned so that he could see the door as well as the window and where his back would be protected by a wall. It was a habit he had developed as a result of previous experiences where meetings with unknown entities hadn't gone as expected.

"Mr. Bower, the reason I called you was to offer you a job. We have a need for someone with your talents and abilities and would like to discuss some business with you. We've checked your background and are impressed with your experience and the quality of work you do. Our office in Hawaii has received some threats and we would like you to look into them and see what you can find out. We'll pay for all travel, hotel accommodations, and provide you with a daily stipend of five hundred dollars, in addition to a daily retainer of one thousand dollars. We'll guarantee you a minimum of sixty days work and a bonus of twenty-five thousand dollars if your work solves the problem. What do you think?" Soliari sat back and waited for his response.

Matt's wheels were spinning in his head, 'this guy just offered me a two month paid vacation in Hawaii, plus a ninety thousand dollar salary and a bonus of twenty-five thousand dollars if I resolve their problem. It's too good to be good, he thought. Sounds like a payoff and a carrot to get me out of town. Why do they want me gone?'

"Well, that sounds quite enticing. I would be stupid to turn such an offer down wouldn't I, no matter what the 'problem' is? Have you discussed your 'problem' in Hawaii with the local police; looked into the investigative talent already there, at probably half the cost?"

"Yes, we've considered these avenues, but to no avail. We want your talents and are willing to pay handsomely for them. Will you consider the offer and let me know by tomorrow afternoon? We need someone to be there by the end of the week if at all possible."

"Mr. Soliari, I'm in the middle of a murder investigation. As handsome as your offer may be I've given my word to help the Sheriff with his problem right now and I never go back on my word."

Soliari looked dumfounded, but caught himself and leaned towards Matt, "Mr. Bower, I think you should take a day or so and consider our offer. It would not be in your best interest to do otherwise."

Matt stared at Soliari for a few seconds then got up from the chair, walked to the door and opened it. He looked back at Soliari and said, "I don't think we need to meet again, Mr. Soliari. You have my decision and I'll determine what's in my best interest, not you or your company", and with that he made his way back to his car.

As soon as Matt had closed Soliari's office door Soliari picked up the phone, dialed an extension, waited for the party to answer and then said, "He didn't take the bait. Do you want me to take care of him even if we have to do it here in Arizona?" He waited for a response then said, "Ok, I'll make it look like an accident; no problem," and then hung up. He then dialed another extension, "Bower is leaving the facility right now. We need to go forward with plan B. Wait until he's on the freeway then make sure he doesn't walk away from the unfortunate accident, got it?" Soliari hung up, then sat back thinking how much easier it would have been if Bower would have taken care of Soliari's other problem before he met his demise. But now, he would personally have to eliminate the source of all the publicity being generated by the 'other problem', the one Bower was working on himself. Just the though of killing made his pulse beat a little bit faster. Like he was about to get a hit of heroin. It made him anxious and edgy. He pulled out a 9 millimeter Smith and Wesson from his shoulder holster and looked down at it, caressing it in his hands. He sat there smiling, "Well baby, no rest for the wicked, eh?"

****

Matt drove out of SafePhoto-RD's facilities thinking about what had just happened, still wondering why they wanted to get him out of town to the tune of ninety thousand dollars and a sixty day vacation in Hawaii! Of course, if he had met with an untimely accident during his stay it wouldn't cost them anything, other than a flight ticket and a one night stay at a hotel, if that. Without thinking, he turned his directional signal on indicating his intention of getting onto the freeway utilizing the long onramp that inclined up about three hundred yards before traffic merged. About two thirds the way up the onramp the back of his head hit the seat's headrest as a large unmarked truck plowed into the back of his car, pushing it towards the edge of the embankment. He accelerated, thinking he could bring his car under control but it was too late. The front right passenger's tire caught the edge of the embankment and steered the car onward, plunging it over the side and careening it out of control tumbling over and over until it reached the bottom. Since it had turned dark, all he could see was a bunch of desert rushing at him as the car rolled down the side of the hill. When it hit the bottom of a ravine running alongside the freeway it came to rest on the passenger side. The airbags had deployed, temporarily pinning him between the seat and the steering wheel. He instinctively reached for the door handle and tried pushing it up and open; it wouldn't budge. His seatbelt was also not releasing so he reached for the knife he always carried in the door's side pocket, cut the belt and pushed himself out the broken window. As he landed, he hit the ground rolling not stopping until he was a good twenty feet from the car. As he lay there, assessing the damage to his body, he saw and heard the rush of dirt tumbling down from above. It was precipitated by a person sliding down the incline, carrying what looked like a small rectangular can. The person, without looking in, quickly doused the car with its contents, then threw something under the car and immediately ran down the ravine and out of sight. Matt instinctively rolled, as fast as he could, further away from the car which, after a few seconds, exploded into oblivion. The air concussion from the massive explosion lifted his body off the ground and threw it further away from the accident. As he lay there, he could hear the sound of a truck starting up and driving off, just above him on the freeway onramp. He got up and looked at the remains of what was once his car, burning furiously, giving off a huge red glow that lit up the night's sky for hundreds of yards in all directions. Matt sat down to wait for the authorities, or someone to assist him. As he sat there he thought, 'well, I guess I was ruder than I thought when I turned down Soliari's offer. Guess I'll have to think of a way to apologize to him, possibly throw him a barbecue myself – maybe in the back seat of his car!'

CHAPTER 10

Chief Arbaugh was sitting in his office looking over a list of names. Fourteen of the names had check marks next to them; the other eight didn't. He looked down and read out loud the next name on the list without a check mark: 'Bob Noble'. He entered the name into his computer and a screen appeared showing all of the citations Mr. Noble had been issued over the past few years, along with his demographic information. Arbaugh printed the information, walked over to the printer, folded the paper it had just ejected, slipped it into his breast pocket, exited the program he had been using and turned the computer off. He then grabbed the keys to his squad car, told dispatch he was checking out for the night, and left the station.

The sheriff's posse car was unmarked and parked two blocks down the street from the El Mora police station's parking lot. Two elderly men sat in the front seat talking about their favorite football teams, while watching for any cars to leave the station. All of a sudden, one of them stopped talking and pointed to the car Arbaugh was driving off in. They both buckled up and took off in pursuit of the Chief's car, cautious not to follow too close. Little did they know that Chief Arbaugh was fully aware of their presence and had allowed them to follow him, until this particular night. He drove to the freeway, put the gas pedal to the floor and hit his lights as if in pursuit of a motorist. The sheriff's deputies were left behind almost immediately and Arbaugh shut off his lights and exited the freeway a few off-ramps down. He then proceeded to the address on the paper he had printed out.

A few hundred yards behind Arbaugh's car was another car, undetected by Arbaugh. The driver was looking at his navigation screen where a blip was registering on what looked like a GPS map. The blip was Arbaugh's car, which had an undetected locator magnetically attached to its frame by the pursuer. Arbaugh continued his route towards his objective, Mr. Noble's residence. When he arrived he noticed there were no lights on in the house so he pulled his car a half block away, shut off the lights and parked, anticipating the arrival of his target. A few minutes went by when a car appeared down the street coming in the direction of the house, but it slowly passed by the house and Arbaugh's car then pulled into a driveway a few houses down the road behind Arbaugh. A few more minutes went by. The night was getting darker. Arbaugh had picked a night when there would be no moon. It always seemed easier for him that way; difficult for witnesses to see anything. He was so intent on watching for his next victim to arrive that he was unaware of the man who had gotten out of the car that had passed him a few minutes earlier. The only indication he had was when he heard a knock on his car's passenger side window and saw a form standing there. He turned on the car key and pressed the button to roll down the window on that side of the car to see who was there. As he moved closer to the window he saw a man standing there, with a business suit on; 'Can I help you', Arbaugh said as he strained to see the man's face.

The man looked into the car at Arbaugh. In an instant his face lit up, as the man pulled the trigger of his silenced 9 millimeter Glock. Arbaugh's body was flung backwards as his head exploded, then slumped over onto the floor of the car. The man reached in the car, placed his gun at the base of Arbaugh's neck and shot him again, then casually walked back to his car and drove off. He reflected back on his thoughts the day before as he drove off, 'just like mainstreaming heroin – what a high!'

The next day when Matt arrived at his office Marcy was ready for him with a barrage of information: "Did you hear about Chief Arbaugh? He's dead! Shot execution style Ciara said, as he was sitting in his car. Looks like he was on a stake out, or something. You need to call Ciara, then the sheriff's office. Oh, by the way, how are you feeling this morning? Any less sore from your ordeal the other day?"

"Will do, thanks Marcy. I feel much better," and Matt went directly to his desk and called Ciara.

"Ciara, its me. What's going on over there; what happened to Arbaugh?"

"Looks like he was executed; a bullet to the face and another to the base of the back of his neck! And by the way, I found a piece of paper in his shirt pocket you'll be extremely interested in. I'm emailing you a copy of it, as I need to turn it into the sheriff, along with his other possessions. It has a man's name on it along with a list of traffic citations he was issued, all in the past few years. And Arbaugh was parked on the street where the guy lives. I bet if you check the name to that list you have it'll be on it."

"Thanks Ciara, will do. Keep me posted on any further developments, will you? Talk to you later this evening. Good by." Matt then opened his email account, found the attachment Ciara had sent him and compared the name to the list and Nobel's name was on it. His hunch about Arbaugh was right; he was the serial killer. But who killed him and why? What was Arbaugh into that had gotten him killed, by a professional none the less. A professional who had been hired to eliminate Arbaugh as a liability of some kind. What did Arbaugh do to make himself a liability? He felt the answer would point him in the direction of Arbaugh's killer and possibly something bigger than what was going on with Arbaugh. And if he was right about the list of potential victims, with the death of Arbaugh it would mean the end of the serial killings. He needed to talk to the sheriff to see what their perspective was on this, and see what they were doing to find the killer of Arbaugh.

"Afternoon Sheriff, I understand Arbaugh is dead; what happened?"

"Matt, good to hear from you. How are you feeling now that you've had a day to recover from your ordeal?"

"Much better. Any information on the truck that was involved in the incident?"

"Only that witnesses said it was a white one, that it pulled over and it looked like a man was rushing down to help out, when a huge blast occurred and he then got back into the truck and drove off. It looks like the evidence indicates he used a can of gas and, believe it or not, a hand grenade to blow up and burn your car. They definitely wanted to make sure you were not going to walk away. Your quick thinking and actions saved your bacon - literally. As for Arbaugh, we're still in the process of gathering crime scene forensics. His dispatch officer said he checked out for the night about forty five minutes prior to his death. We don't know what he was doing where he was found. It looks like he was sitting in his car like he was waiting for something or someone. He gave my deputies the slip or we may have been able to save him; any thoughts?"

"You know that list of potential victims we've been working on. Well, one of the names on the list lives three houses down from where Arbaugh was parked, on the opposite side of the street. And in Arbaugh's shirt pocket was found a sheet of paper with that name on it, along with a list of ticket citations and his demographic information. I suspect that if you go to Arbaugh's house you'll find an arsenal that will include the guns used in the killings we've been investigating, as well as a few knives; one of which will also match the wounds in the victim's bodies. I'm almost sure our serial killer has been found, eliminated for some reason that I need to find out. I hate to say this, but I think the case of the 'Speed Trap' murders is just the tip of an ice berg we haven't yet discovered. I'll write all this up Sheriff and send it to you by tomorrow. Keep me posted on any further findings. Talk to you later."

****

Johnson had worked for Soliari for about a year now doing odd jobs, running errands, and doing a bit of strong arm work when needed. When Soliari had called him a week earlier to discuss Matt Bower and plan the accident that was to get rid of him, he felt confident all would go well and Soliari's problem would be eliminated. Everything had gone as planned Johnson thought, until he received a call from Soliari asking him to meet at a remote building on the twenty-five acre compound where Soliari worked at nine that evening. He had been told it was to 'settle up', but Johnson felt uneasy about the meeting. All Soliari needed to do if he wanted to 'settle up' with him would be to call him down to Soliari's office and pay him the ten thousand dollars they had agreed on. So Johnson opened his closet, reached for a box on an upper shelf, placed it on the coffee table of his apartment and sat down on the couch. He sat there for a few moments staring at the box thinking of what might transpire in the next few hours. Then he opened the box, reached inside and pulled out a HK45 semi automatic handgun with a night sight and three ten round magazines, one of which he inserted into the gun. The other two he stuffed into a large pocket on the side of his pants. He also pulled out a six shot 38 special S&W revolver with a two inch barrel and bobbed hammer, along with a ranger ankle holster and a box of shells. He loaded the revolver, inserted it into the holster and strapped it to the inside of his left ankle. He then pulled out an IWB holster, lifted up his shirt, clipped it to his pants at the small of his back and holstered the HK45 in it. Finally, he removed from the box a 4.45 inch double edge auto knife that he was very adept at using due to his mercenary training and background. He now felt that he was ready for his meeting with Soliari, hoping he would not need to use any of the weapons but deep inside he knew that was probably not going to be the case. Now, all he could do was sit back and wait until it was time to leave for his meeting with Soliari.

Soliari hung the phone up after he told Johnson about the meeting. It was six o'clock at night. He needed to get to the building that sat on the back five acres behind the main building where his office was and 'prepare' for the meeting with Johnson. Johnson had served his purpose but now he was expendable. He had failed and as Soliari's boss had said numerous times, failure is not an option! Johnson should have stayed at the scene and made sure Bower was dead, and he didn't. He wasn't even sure Johnson knew Bower was still alive but that didn't make any difference; he had failed. When Soliari arrived at the building he began setting up the trap, a trap that no one so far had escaped. Once the prey was in the building, it would never leave alive.

End Episode 1

Episode 2

Internal Combustion

In episode two Matt continues on in the investigation of SafePhoto-RD which leads him to its Board of Directors, James Vardon. Matt is enlisted by the CIA to follow Vardon and find out what he's planning that may have negative worldwide implications. He follows Vardon to Istanbul and finds out that a new weapon is being developed that will have the potential of killing one, or thousands of people, without being traced to its source. Five nations, all adversaries of the United States, are interested in bidding for the technology. Matt must find where the weapon is being developed, obtain a copy of the plans for the CIA, then destroy the facility.

P R O L O G U E

Don Soliari was sitting at his desk when the phone rang; it was his boss: "Good morning Mr. Vardon, what can I...," and before he could say another word he was cut off.

"You bungling ass. I told you we wanted Bower eliminated, and you guaranteed it would be done! We don't tolerate mistakes. You know that. You weren't chosen because we liked your looks. Do you know what magnitude of risk Matt Bower poses to our worldwide operation? You may think he's small potatoes but I guarantee you he has more intelligence in his little finger than you do in your whole body! I don't care if you have to kidnap his mother to get him, just do it. And no more mistakes, do you understand?" The phone went dead in Soliari's hand.

Soliari gingerly placed the phone receiver in its cradle. His face was ashen in color; almost white. Perspiration started to drip from his brow which made him uneasy. He dabbed at it with his handkerchief and visualized in his mind his hands around Bower's neck, squeezing the life out of him. The thought brought color back to his face, a crimson color. This job now became personal. Just like Chief Arbaugh only he would get more pleasure out of killing Bower than he did Arbaugh. He would make him suffer. Nothing at all like Arbaugh. He wondered if Bower would be foolish enough to take another meeting with him. He would call him and see if a trap could be set. Even better, possibly find someone or something Bower cherished enough to put himself in harms way. He would start working on it immediately. Surely Bower had an Achilles heel that would precipitate his demise. Don Soliari would show his employers he was up to any assignment they presented him, that they could depend on him to fulfill his destiny with the company. Their 'go to' man in the field when they needed someone eliminated. That was his ultimate goal.

CHAPTER 11

James Vardon, chairman of the board of SafePhoto-RD, was sitting in his office located on the 66th floor of '70 Pine Street' building in Manhattan, New York, as he slammed the phone down. He peered out of the windows and could see all of Manhattan below and thought, 'power is everything; without it you're nothing. Yet, one little piss-ant person in a piss-ant town like Phoenix, Arizona is somehow diminishing my ability to control the situation, and it's causing the powers above me to take notice. I can't have that happening'.

Although the corporation, SafePhoto-RD, provided a significant amount of positive cash flow to the 'Organization' it was a very small part of the whole. He needed to nip this problem in the bud as soon as possible, or his head would be the next to roll! He had bigger fish to catch. He picked up the phone, pressed speed dial, then the numbers 9-0, and waited for a few seconds as the connection was made to a phone somewhere in Istanbul.

"This is XB-90, confirm please," the voice said as the connection was made.

Vardon responded, "VJ-69 DROP 44; I have an immediate assignment for you. You'll be contacted at 2200 hours tomorrow with your instructions. Do you understand?"

"XB-90 confirms; will be waiting," and then Vardon heard the phone go dead. He then made another phone call to the Chief Operations Officer of SafePhoto-RD in Phoenix and instructed him to provide 'XB-90' with anything he needed, if he should be contacted by him in the next 72 hours. Vardon then opened a laptop sitting on his desk, clicked an icon, and waited for it to open an encryption application. He then proceeded to type in his instructions to XB-90, finished by entering the destination number for it to be sent and the time for it to be transmitted. He re-read what he had typed: 'Terminate with extreme prejudice Matt Bower – Phoenix, Arizona. Terminate Phoenix operative D. Soliari and destroy all files associated with his work at SP-RD. Usual fee of 50k Euro each. End.' He then clicked 'Send' and closed the laptop.

He picked up the phone again and made a direct call to Washington, DC.

"Senator Paul Markham's office, may I help you?"

"Mr. Vardon calling for the senator."

"Oh, yes Mr. Vardon. I'll put you right through; just a moment please." A few seconds later the senator spoke into the phone.

"Yes Jim, what can I do for you?"

"Paul, that legislation in Arizona…..we need to have it passed by the end of next month or it will mean six more cities will not be renewing their contracts with SP; an eight million dollar loss of revenue!" He then hung up, not giving the senator an opportunity to respond. He sat back in his chair, swiveled around to peer out of the windows again and then said out loud, "Power IS everything"!

At 2200 hours, a man in Istanbul opened his laptop and read Vardon's message. He then closed it, unlocked a drawer in his desk and retrieved a passport, a stack of U.S. currency, and a brand new 'throw away' cell phone. He picked up the phone, called a number that connected him to the captain of a private jet owned by the 'Triad Corporation', the parent conglomerate of SafePhoto-RD, and booked a direct flight to Phoenix, Arizona. He then moved to a wall where a large Persian rug was hanging and pushed in on its lower right corner. The rug moved upwards, exposing an arsenal of various and sundry weapons. He removed a number of items and placed them in a carry-on case, then left for the airport. The plane, a Gulfstream G550, was to leave in exactly an hour if all went as planned, and he would be in Arizona in fourteen hours. He figured the job shouldn't take him more than a day or two to complete, and he would be 100k Euros richer and back in Istanbul smoking his favorite tobacco from his 'nargile' pipe. What a life, he thought. He had no compunction taking a life if it would keep him from the slums he had grown up in. He would do anything to make sure that would never happen! Just two more targets, Bower and Soliari, and he could retire from the employ of this infidel company named 'Triad XB'!

CHAPTER 12

It had been almost forty-eight hours since Soliari had been chastised by his boss, but he believed he had found a way to eliminate Matt Bower once and for all. Going through all of the information accumulated on Bower, he felt he had found two of Matt's weaknesses: Ciara Caddell his love interest, and Marcy, his office assistant. He would use one of them to lure Matt into a trap and then eliminate them both. He called the County coroner's office and asked to speak to the assistant coroner.

"This is Ms. Caddell, may I help you?"

"Ms. Caddell, this is the Super from your building. I'm sorry to disturb you but I wanted you to know that a water pipe broke in your apartment today. It leaked through to the apartment below and they called us for help."

"What condition is my place in; did it destroy anything?"

"I'm afraid so. Could you come to your apartment now so we can move your belongings to another apartment temporarily, until we get things cleaned up; it will only take a day or so. We just need you to be here before we touch any of your belongings."

"Yes, of course. I'll leave now and be there in a half hour. Thank you for calling."

Soliari had made the phone call to Ciara in the parking structure that housed Ciara's car. Ten minutes had passed before Ciara arrived at her car. Her mind was reeling with so many thoughts: where would she stay, will she need to temporarily store things, how will this impact her time at work, etc. She had not remembered what Matt had told her about being aware of her surroundings, and did not suspect anything as the well dressed man approached her from the side, just as she unlocked her car door.

"Ms. Caddell?"

"Yes."

"Do you know a Matt Bower?"

"Yes, what's happened; who are you?"

Soliari stepped forward so that he was only inches from Ciara, and poked his gun into her side: "If you'll go with me quietly, nothing will happen to you, or Mr. Bower. Do you understand?"

Ciara stared into the man's eyes and was shocked for a moment, then composed herself; "Where is Matt, what have you done to him?"

"Head towards that car over there! And no sudden moves! I would hate to have to do something we would both regret, along with Bower. Now move!" And with that he violently pushed her towards his car.

When they had gotten into the car, Soliari asked Ciara to call Matt from her cell phone. When Matt answered, Soliari took the phone and said: "Mr. Bower, how nice to speak to you again. Ms. Caddell and I would like you to meet us at the following address in fifteen minutes. If we don't see you, Ms. Caddell's associate at the coroner's office will be examining her within the hour, do you understand?"

Matt immediately recognized Soliari's voice, "I understand Soliari. Don't touch a hair of her head or you'll regret it for the rest of your short life, you scum bag!" – Soliari hung up after giving Matt the location he was to meet them at. Matt was at his office and it would take him all of fifteen minutes to get to where Soliari had instructed him to go. It was almost dark but the place was familiar to Matt, since he had been within the vicinity on another case and he knew it to be empty of any businesses or residences. It was a place where trucking companies use to reside, prior to the economic downturn. When Matt arrived, he pulled his car into the large complex of empty shipping warehouses, and stopped for a minute. He thought he had seen movement in his rear view mirror, but as he tried to spot where it had come from, he couldn't. So he slowly drove onward, past the first set of buildings, then on to the next all the while checking his rear view mirror.

Soliari and his hostage were sitting in Soliari's car half way down the wide thoroughfare that was skirted on both sides by the buildings. He had parked so that the car was two-thirds way turned towards one set of buildings, providing a shield between them and Matt's approaching car.

Matt slowly coasted his car towards Soliari's and immediately his cell phone rang. It was Soliari again: "What do you want Soliari."

"I want you to get out of your car and walk towards us. No abrupt movements or Ms. Caddell here will no longer be among the living, do you understand?"

"That's not going to happen Soliari. I step out and we're both dead. You and I both know that. You've placed us in a Mexican stand-off! You let Ms. Caddell walk away from the car and as soon as she's out of range, say the end of that building in front of you, then we'll both move out into the open; me first. It can't work any other way as far as I'm concerned."

"Start walking Ms. Caddell, and for Bower's and your sake don't look back or stop, understand?" and Soliari nudged Ciara forward with the muzzle of his gun. "Ok Bower, she's on her way."

Matt waited until Ciara was at a safe distance until he moved from one side of his car to the other, opening the passenger's door as he did so, giving him some protection from Soliari's position. "Ok Soliari I made the first move, now start walking towards me and I'll do the same."

Matt saw Soliari start to move towards him, while raising his gun for a shot at Matt. Matt took a lunge forward and to the side, hoping to use his car as a black backdrop, so Soliari wouldn't have a clear shot. As Matt hit the pavement a shot rang out and Soliari's body jerked backwards towards his car. A split second later Soliari's head exploded into a thousand pieces as another bullet followed.

Matt instinctively rolled towards his car as a third shot followed the first two. This time though the bullet just missed Matt's head. Matt moved behind one of the wheels of the car and, leaning up against it, cautiously looked through one of the windows. Another shot slammed into the windshield and smashed Matt's window, just missing him again. Matt saw the muzzle flash this time and knew where the shooter had positioned himself. The shooter moved swiftly to another location not thinking Matt would see him, but he did. A second later, taking dead aim, Matt's 45 belched fire and the 155 grain hollow point slammed into the shooter's torso jerking it upwards in a macabre motion. Matt swiftly moved into a couching position leveling his gun at the target. Again the Glock spewed forth its deadly projectiles, and again the form was thrown back into the darkness.

Matt cautiously moved towards the seemingly immobile form and at that moment his mind flashed back to the time he had shot the assailant in DC assuming he had killed him, only to find out differently. With that in his mind, he kept his gun pointed towards the unmoving form as he slowly approached it. He peered down at the lifeless body of what looked like a foreigner, possibly of Turkish descent. The only distinguishing mark Matt could make out was a tattoo on his arm just above his left wrist. It read - XB-90!

Matt could hear running coming from behind him and as he turned around Ciara slammed into his body, her arms encircling his neck, kisses flying everywhere!

"Oh Matt, Matt, I thought you were going to be killed. Are you alright? What happened?"

"I think we just witnessed a reversal of fortunes, with the prospective beneficiaries loosing out."

That night, a Gulfstream G550 jet took off from Phoenix in route to Istanbul. The pilot made a call to New York: "Mr. Vardon, you asked me to call when we were on our way back to Istanbul. We just left Phoenix, however, the passenger is not aboard."

"Thank you. That will be all." Vardon slowly replaced the phone in its cradle on his desk. His face was a bit ashen in color; his mouth a bit dry. If he didn't hear from XB-90 in the next twenty-four hours he would have to implement plan 'B' immediately, before the powers above him implemented their own plans. Plans he was sure that would include him, as well as Bower, this time.

CHAPTER 13

Two days had past since Matt's ordeal with Soliari and the unknown sniper. He was sitting in his office when Marcy came in and said two men from the CIA were there to see him.

"Mr. Bower, my name is agent Harris. This is agent Abrams. We have some information on that man you killed last week. Could we have some of your time to discuss it?"

"I've been waiting to hear about that. Sit down."

"The government has been interested for a long time in a worldwide organization called 'Triad XB'. It has over a hundred different corporations under its control, most of them fronts for clandestine operations. We believe the man who tried to kill you, who you killed, worked for Triad XB as a professional assassin sent here to eliminate you and Mr. Soliari. Mr. Soliari because he failed to get rid of you, and you because you had become suspicious about one of their cash cows, SafePhoto-RD. We want you to help us destroy Triad XB and its operations. How would you feel about that?"

"How can I help? What do you propose I do?"

"We want you to find out as much as you can about SafePhoto-RD; who they're paying off and how they're keeping a hold on the market here in Arizona. We're in hopes that, as you investigate them, you'll ultimately bump into Triad XB and be able to find out what part they play in supporting any nefarious activities carried on by SafePhoto-RD. We would act a support team to your efforts, and the government will pay you generously for your talents and time. Will you work with us, Mr. Bower?"

"Triad XB is behind all of this? Soliari, Arbaugh, and the Turkish assassin? If it leads to getting rid of SafePhoto-RD with their speed traps, 'eyes in the sky', and the dirty legislators who line the pockets of local politicians to obtain contracts for their services, yes, I'll help. Who knows, we may find bigger fish to fry somewhere in the great corporate offices in the sky!"

The phone buzzed on Mr. Vardon's desk. He knew who was calling and opened one of his desk drawers as he picked up the receiver. He looked down into the drawer. At the bottom lay a small caliber handgun. "Yes, sir, what can I do for you sir?" As he spoke perspiration started to form on his forehead and he could also feel it dripping from his underarms.

The voice on the other end of the phone was Vardon's superior, the head of Triad XB. Of course, most of the time Vardon felt he had no superiors; he was obsessed with power. But he was also a pragmatist, most of the time.

And it was pragmatic of him to recognize his superior as just that --- 'superior'! He was now being told that although the Arizona fiasco was embarrassing, to say the least, it should not stop the wheels that had already been put in place to move the operation forward. Senator Markham was to have all necessary resources to assure passage of the legislation in Arizona, as well as in Colorado. County contracts of each state were to be aggressively pursued and finalized by the end of the year for the coming three years. It was critical for the next phase of the project to go forward and that this be accomplished. Vardon was to be personally responsible for the success of the endeavor; there would be no excuses for failure this time!

Vardon hung up the phone, after giving reassurances and promises to his boss. He looked at the desk drawer he had opened previous to the phone call, with the gun in it, and quickly closed it with a sigh of relief. He would live to fight another day he thought.

He placed a call to Phoenix, to talk to his undercover contact there: "Hello Ray, I just spoke to VJ-00. I'm sending you an encrypted message that will provide you with access to funds for securing the votes necessary to get that damned bill passed, and to get all the County contracts renewed. I cannot stress enough to you that failure is not an option; this is our last chance. Do you understand?"

The voice on the other end talked for a few minutes then Vardon said, "Good, I'm sure that will work Ray. Success will mean upward mobility for you, and firmer ground for me. Good luck."

Two weeks later the legislation required to support photo radar in Arizona passed and the contracts were signed. Vardon again sat back in the plush oversized executive chair in his great corporate office in the sky. Looking out over the city below he repeated the mantra 'power is everything'. And then he thought of VJ-00; yes, power IS everything!

CHAPTER 14

After meeting with the two CIA agents and obtaining all the information they had on SafePhoto-RD Matt took a few days and mapped out a plan that he felt would expose the company's involvement in political corruption through bribery, extortion and graft; the purpose of which was to facilitate their criminal actions. He felt that if he could isolate the specific way in which RD was able to benefit from the County contracts, that was not legitimate, he could expose the whole industry. Doing this would necessitate finding someone who was intimately familiar with how the underbelly of the industry worked, and he thought he knew just the person; Manny Lansky!

Manny Lansky was currently in a federal penitentiary in Otisville, New York. He had been fingered as an insider to the nation's most infamous Ponzi scheme but was instrumental in cutting an 'under the table' deal with the law which led to the capture and conviction of a number of Wall Street hoods, underworld bosses and politicians back in 2005. For this, his sentence was reduced to 15 years at a minimum security prison with the possibility of parole after nine. Since it was his third strike he felt lucky to cut the deal. And the prison served kosher food and regular access to a rabbi. What more could a Jewish prisoner want! Even though Manny was up for parole in a short while it was no guarantee that he would get out. If Matt could swing it to get Manny paroled early, with Matt assigned as his 'parole officer', he could assist in making Matt's plan work. Manny knew how things worked in the political corruption arena and he was a corporate lawyer to boot. Just the man Matt needed to crack this case wide open. And he knew Matt would be on the up-and-up with him, since Matt helped him get the lighter sentence.

Marcy was sitting at her computer, working on a software program she had devised to download data to a database she had built, when the outside office door opened and an impeccably dressed older man walked in. He stood approximately five foot four, weighed about one hundred forty pounds soaking wet, about fifty-eight years young and his clothes were tailored, but a few years behind the current fashion; say twenty!

"Can I help you?"

"I'm here to see Mr. Bower. He's expecting me I believe."

"And your name is?"

"Emmanuel Lansky. My friends call me Manny. And yours sweetheart?"

Marcy's eyebrow rose as she got up and moved towards Matt's door, "Matt's expecting you Mr. Lansky; my name is Marcy. This way please."

Matt was waiting for Manny and after a few minutes of social talk they got down to business. "Manny, we'll be working under the umbrella of the CIA; you'll be working undercover. This job, if we're successful, could change your life and mine forever. But it'll be dangerous. If you're found out it could mean your life. I know we discussed it a little bit when you were in prison but now it's necessary for you to know the level of danger involved." Matt went on and told Manny about the attempt on his life.

"If you feel you don't want to go forward I understand; it's your call."

"Are you kidding? I have a chance to be absolved of my past sins, to be involved in something that'll help our country, to give back a small portion of what I took? No matter how dangerous it is Matt, I'm in! When do we start?"

"We start now, with Senator Paul Markham!"

****

Senator Markham's office was impressive to say the least. It had that 'old world' look; hunter green, real leather, gold accent pieces. It even came with a 'hot and cold' running secretary; hot looks and cold stare!

"Senator Markham, there's a man here to see you regarding some mutual friends? His name is Mr. Emmanual Lansky. Do you want to see him or shall I set up an appointment?"

"Find out what mutual friends Doris."

"He said you would want to talk to him directly for that information."

"Tell him I'm busy. I don't know any Lansky....wait!" The senator's mind flashed the name Lansky in bright lights; he recognized it - - corporate attorney for Fairmont Securities. A major player in corporate securities a number of years back. "Doris, show Mr. Lansky in would you."

"Thank you Senator for seeing me on such short notice. My old friend Senator Walburt, god rest his soul, said that if I ever was in Arizona I should look you up. And I believe you also know Vern Ormond, David Ackerman, and Jim Vardon?"

The Senator extended his hand to Manny, "Yes, yes of course. And I believe I have heard of you; corporate attorney, right?"

"'Retired' corporate attorney, Senator. I'm in the process of moving to Arizona for my health, and to possibly be of assistance to some of my friends in the East, if you know what I mean."

"Actually I don't know what you mean. Please explain if you would."

"Contracts. My expertise is in developing and closing on contracts that are designed to enhance the position of my employers, of course. Some of my previous acquaintances are interested in doing business out of Arizona. They feel it has a 'progressive' attitude towards big business; large corporations who are not adverse to investing in the State. It is my understanding that you too might be willing to assist in developing business enterprises in Arizona. Is that correct?"

The senator felt uneasy about answering that question for some reason. "Mr. Lansky, Arizona welcomes and encourages business development within the state. How do you come to know James Vardon, if I may ask?"

"A number of years back I was hired by one of his holding companies, Fairmont Securities, to develop contracts between large investors. The company made billions and Mr. Vardon was very happy with the work. I haven't been in touch for quite a while. In fact, I don't even know if he's still alive! During my tenure as a contract consultant your name came up a number of times. I just thought Vardon's name would be one you might remember. A shot in the dark you might say. Just like Ormond and Ackerman; just acquaintances."

"Mr. Lansky, why don't you give me your phone number and where you're staying and I'll get back to you. I may have some work for you after all. Let me check a few things out and maybe we can do some business together." The senator stood and extended his hand to Manny, "I'll be in touch, one way or another."

"Looking forward to hearing from you senator, and call me Manny, Paul."

"Sure, sure. Have a good day ..... Manny."

Manny knew the senator would be checking up on him and had given him names who he knew were no longer among the living, except Vardon's. And that would check out, since Vardon was a key player in the Ponzi scheme that made his company billions. And he was sure Vardon wouldn't exactly remember the time he had rubbed elbows with Manny since it was only once, and Manny had held a 'behind the scenes' position; one that Vardon would definitely understand. The CIA had taken care of his prison record so it looked like Manny had dropped off the earth for the past nine years. The senator and Vardon would appreciate that aspect of his background. All he could do now was to wait for the senator's call. Hopefully it would be a call, and not a bullet to the back of the head!

Manny reported back to Matt as to how things went with the senator. Two days later a knock at his apartment door interrupted him from his meal. He had been waiting for a call; a knock at his door was not expected. It may be Matt he thought, but that was very unlikely since he had just talked to Matt two hours previously. As he approached the door he knew it might be a risk to look through the peep hold and get a bullet right in the eye; POW! He would never even hear it he thought. Only the sight of a gun muzzle staring back at him. That was the risk he had to take. It was the type of life he had chosen years ago. When he peered thru the door he saw a large, well dressed man standing there. Manny opened the door.

"Mr. Lansky. My name is Dave. I work for the senator. Would you like to follow me; he's waiting in the parking garage. He'd like to talk to you."

"Of course, of course. Let me get my jacket and I'll be ready." Manny stepped back into his apartment, retrieved the coat that Matt had wired with a GPS tracker button and recorder, activated the button, slipped it on, then followed the man to where the senator was waiting.

"Senator, good to see you again", Manny said as he started to enter the stretched limo.

"Mr. Lansky, I hope you don't mind if Dave pats you down. Just to be safe you might say."

"No, no of course not. I understand." Manny was cool, but he could feel the butterflies in his stomach, hoping the lapel button and recording pen were not discovered as such!

"He's clean senator," Dave said then closed the car door, opened the other door at the front of the limo, and climbed in. A smoked glass partition kept the front seat passengers from seeing or hearing what transpired in the back of the limo.

"Manny, good to see you again. Sorry for the precautions but business is business and some is more confidential than others. It seems your background check is as you said. Mr. Vardon does remember you, slightly. Of course, being in the background as the corporate attorney you didn't have many opportunities to socialize."

"It's one of the perks of the job, if you know what I mean. What can I do for you senator? I'm anxious to get working out here and get settled."

"An important piece of legislation just passed and becomes law in sixty days. Once it does, we're already in line with County RFP's; they're shoe-in's. We have the people in our pockets that make the decisions in each County. We need to have you look through the contracts we'll be having them sign and see how we can incorporate language that will allow a company named SafePhoto-RD to extract data from their databases for 'analysis purposes'. That will then allow access to their servers to massage the metadata as needed. We also want you to work with our people to assure those who make the purchase decisions for the counties are bound to do so with RD; possibly massage their mortgage contracts, etc. Do you understand?"

"Yes, I believe I do. What's my cut and when do you want me to begin?"

The senator pushed an intercom button and told Dave to roll down the partition window and hand him 'the bag'. "We'll pay you in cash. Here is your first installment; one will be provided each month. Dave will bring you everything you need to begin work. If you need anything else just let him know. He'll be your contact; you and I will never meet again Mr. Lansky. Good-by."

At that point in the conversation the car door opened and Dave was standing there. Manny exited the car with the bag of cash and watched as the senator's car slowly made its way out of the hotel's garage. The next day Dave showed up at Manny's hotel room with a box full of folders; each one marked with the name of a County. A master file held the contracts that each were to sign. Those would be what he was expected to review and improve, as the senator specified. He contacted Matt using the GPS button; turning it on meant he was to be followed from the position he was at. Since he would be staying in his hotel room Matt would contact him there after ten minutes of no movement.

Matt went to the concierge of Manny's hotel and picked up a package that contained the recording of the Senator and Manny that had taken place in the limo two days previous. After listening to it with his CIA operatives they all agreed it was very incriminating, but of course they needed to get to Vardon and his operation, not just the senator. Waiting for contracts to be consummated and rounding up crooked County administrators would take a long time. They would pass that off to another team that would work with Manny going forward.

Matt and the CIA felt he needed to concentrate on getting Vardon and those behind him. Bringing SafePhoto-RD down would now be a job for the new team; Manny was in good hands.

What was burned into Matt's mind was the tattoo 'XB-90' on the assassin's arm and the name of Vardon's conglomerate, 'Triad XB'. There was a connection there, and he guessed that the orders to the assassin came from Vardon. Now all he had to do was figure out how to confirm it and make it stick. And since Vardon's 'nest' was in New York, that's where Matt felt he needed to be; plucking out some high flying feather!

CHAPTER 15

The flight from Phoenix to LaGuardia took five hours. When Matt arrived at LaGuardia a good friend of his was waiting for him. He had met, and worked with, Vern Reden while a homicide detective in DC. Vern was a no frills kind of guy, one Matt truly enjoyed being around. Vern had served in the Viet Nam War and had retired from the Marines after twenty years with the rank of a Lieutenant Colonel. He went in just after college and decided it was his way of life. Now, he too had gotten into the PI business and knew the ropes well.

"How are you doing on this FINE marine corps day!?"

"OUTSTANDING!" was Vern's reply; a grin as big as a house covering his face.

"Ooh-Rah, Devil Dog!", Matt continued.

"Ooh-Rah, Leatherneck!", and Vern grabbed Matt in a big bear hug way then ushered him to a car that was waiting for them just off the tarmac, a privilege given to only a few at LaGuardia.

Once installed in the car and all the normal pleasantries were exchanged Vern got down to the business at hand, "So, what's the mission Major, where to first."

Matt brought Vern up to speed on what had transpired with SafePhoto-RD, how the CIA had asked Matt to be part of their team, and that the mission now was to find out as much as they could about James Vardon without Vardon knowing about it just yet: where he lived, places he frequented, acquaintances he associated with and such. Initially it would be a 'reconnaissance' mission, hopefully followed by a 'search and destroy' mission! It would be dangerous because Vardon was a very powerful man and with power came dangerous resources. The CIA expected Matt to determine how Vardon linked to the Triad conglomerate and what part he played in the overall scheme of things. They needed to find out the chain of command, if possible, and where the headquarters of Triad XB was and who, or what, ran it.

The CIA had rented an apartment for Matt in a hotel close to where Vardon's building was so he and Vern set up shop immediately. It wasn't the Ritz but in New York just about any hotel was above par by most people's standards. They both reconnoitered the place and its surroundings, making note of the ingress and egress points, windows, exits, elevators, where the hotel staff's work area/rooms were located on the floor, etc. After a while a knock at their door brought them both to attention, but it was only the staff delivering their bags to the room. Additional bags, sent by his CIA operative, were later delivered. They contained electronic surveillance paraphernalia specifically ordered by Matt and Vern.

Over the next few days he and Vern 'shadowed' Vardon and utilized technology to track his movements and listen in on his phone conversations. They set up an office in a building directly across from where Vardon worked, where they could watch and hear his every move. As a result, they became aware of a meeting he was going to hold with a number of 'associates' the next night. It would be just east of the Bronx, close to Eastchester Bay, in a private enclave of estate homes called 'The Country Club'.

"We have to call in some help for this one Vern. The CIA will need to provide us with the means to infiltrate the meeting so we can take pictures of those attending and capture any conversations of interest. There's not enough lead time for us to set this up ourselves."

"I agree but since the meeting will be close to the bay I think we should have a back-up plan just in case the CIA drops the ball. I have access to a boat that we can use to carry some gear and be ready for a get-away if necessary. I'll have it standing by at Cherry Tree Point, which is about two blocks from where the meeting is going to be held. It's going to be a full moon tonight so we shouldn't have any problems finding our way around if necessary. What do you think?"

"I think it's a great idea because if things go sideways we'll need to NOT depend on the CIA to bail us out. Let's start the ball rolling," and with that Matt called his CIA operative and told him of the meeting and their plan to photo and record as much as they could, but excluded Vern's back-up plan. Vern placed a few calls and the boat was arranged. It would be well equipped with weaponry and plenty of fuel just in case it was needed for more than just a quick get-away and would be docked, and in position, by 8pm the next night.

The CIA quickly went to work and found the catering service that would be handling the meeting and 'replaced' it with their own crew and vehicle, equipped with surveillance and communications. They then met with Matt and Vern the next morning and equipped them with on-person cameras and audio receivers that were 'seemingly' undetectable by security wands. Three of their agents would act as employees of the catering service while Matt and Vern would work to chart the layout of the building and position themselves to see and hear what transpired. The catering service was to arrive four hours in advance of the meeting, so that would give them plenty of time to do their job.

The catering van pulled up to the estate at exactly 3:45pm with Matt, Vern and three CIA agents inside. The estate was enclosed by a twelve foot high electrified metal fence. The guards at the gates checked their ID cards and passed the van through, telling them where to park and unload. As the van slowly pulled through the gates and onto the grounds of the estate Matt looked back at the fence and said to Vern, "that could be an issue if we need to get out of here in a hurry." He also noticed, when one of the guards turned to go back into the guard shack and his coat flew open, that under it he was carrying a machine gun called a 'Micro Uzi' which fired 9 millimeter parabellum bullets. Rather overkill, Matt thought, for a gate guard!

Matt and Vern went to work immediately after they exited the van. They checked the layout of the building, how many staff was there, and the location of all the exits. They then covertly placed their surveillance cameras and audio 'bugs' where they would provide the most coverage.

At around 7pm a limousine pulled up to the house and six scantily, but well dressed, 'call girls' stepped out of the car. They were greeted by a woman in a business suit who introduced herself as Gabrielle. Gabrielle was well proportioned and walked with an athleticism that belied abilities that surpassed just taking notes and making coffee! She ushered the women into the house and up the stairs to a large room prepared for their use. Within the room were a number of doors, each leading to another small room laid out to accommodate 'overnight' guests. Once the ladies were settled in Gabrielle told the girls they would be expected downstairs at exactly nine-thirty, where each would introduce themselves to one of the men in attendance; to be their 'escort' for the night if the men elected to stay. They were to be cleaned up and ready to leave at ten in the morning at which time the limousine would take them back to their place of origin. She then excused herself and went to her room at the end of a long hallway.

Once Matt and Vern had finished their work placing the surveillance equipment, they set up shop in the attic. A small laptop from one of their bags was extracted so they could monitor all of the cameras and audio equipment that they had placed. It was getting dark so they reconnoitered the attic room. It had a pivotal portal window at one end and a small access door to the roof at the other. A 'panic' key was programmed into the laptop to warn the CIA agents posing as the catering staff. If used it meant they had been discovered and it was every man for himself.

They settled in to wait for the arrival of Vardon and his entourage, whoever that might be.

It hadn't been more than ten minutes when they heard some vehicles arriving at the front of the house. They looked out of the portal window and two large vans pulled up. The back doors flew open and five men from each bailed out. They were all dressed in black suits, ties, gloves and white shirts. Slung across their shoulders was an IWI X95 flattop machine gun which they immediately hid, as much as possible, under their coats. They all gathered at the front of the lead vehicle where a tall, well built, white haired man was exiting. He gave them instructions and each of the men immediately proceeded to move towards their assigned 'stations' for the night.

Matt went over to the laptop and one of the duffel bags, pulled out a map of the building and handed Vern a pencil, instructing him to mark down the position of each man stationed around the house. The clock on the laptop indicated 8pm and darkness filled the room. He then turned on a small battery powered lantern which gave off just enough light to make out their immediate surroundings. The sound of other vehicles arriving propelled Matt to the window, while Vern kept a watch on the laptop.

Two exceptionally long limousines were pulling up just as Matt peered out.

"Vern, come here," Matt whispered, as one of the doors of the trailing limousine opened and six men began to disembark. "Do you recognize any of them?"

Vern looked down at the group of men. His eyes grew wide and then he whispered, "What in the 'hell' have we gotten ourselves into Matt. I can't believe who we're seeing here!"

Just as Matt was about to say something a door of the leading limo opened and out stepped James Vardon who hesitated for a moment, looked around, then gave a slight tip of his head indicating to someone inside it was safe to leave the confines of the car.

A small, rotund form of a man worked his way out of the car and slowly moved past Vardon and into the house, not waiting for the others to follow. He was dressed in a furry full length coat, large wide brimmed Borsalino felt hat pulled down on his head, dark red gloves and shoes, and brandished a cane in his left hand, one that looked as if it were made of gold.

"I've never seen the short one before," Vern said as if in awe, "but the others: the first one is the first vice-president of economics and foreign affairs to the president of Iran, the second is the vice-secretary general of the communist party of Viet Nam and a first cousin to the president of North Korea, the third is the chief assistant to the prime minister of Russia, the fourth I do not know, the fifth is first assistant vice-chancellor of Germany and the sixth is," and Matt interrupted Vern with, "vice-chairman of the US senate appropriations committee!"

"My God!", Vern responded in a dejected tone as they both turned and walked back to the laptop and small lantern, whose light felt like it was the only thing in the room that radiated some glimmer of hope. As they sat there thinking to themselves Vern pointed to the laptop's screen and to an image on one of the surveillance cameras.

"Quick, take cover," Matt whispered as he clicked off the lantern and closed the laptop. They both moved swiftly into the darkness of the attic. One of the 'men in black', the grey haired one, was approaching the attic door off the hallway. Another was twenty or thirty paces behind him, just standing there.

The attic door slowly opened and the leader of the guards stood at the bottom of the stairs listening, staring up into the darkness. Matt and Vern crouched in silence waiting for his next move which was to un-holster a silenced Walther PP and slowly ascend the stairs. Crouching at the top, he surveyed the darkness of the room. The only light was from the window at the other end of the attic. The moon was full and cast a beam across the room that caught the surface of the laptop, creating a small glimmer. He saw the slight glimmer, stood up and moved towards it. As he approached and reached for it, Vern and Matt both moved as one. Vern grabbed his gun hand from behind and wrapped his left arm and hand around the man's shoulder and mouth. Matt grabbed the front of his shirt with his left hand and drove his right, which held a five inch knife, into the man's upper solar plexus once, and then again. The man dropped like a sack of potatoes; dead before he touched the floor. Vern grabbed the man's gun and tucked it under his belt in the small of his back.

Both men looked at each other, waiting in silence, hoping their sounds and actions went unnoticed. Some footsteps were heard running down the hallway, away from the attic door. They reached for the laptop, opened it and pressed the 'warning' key that would notify the CIA agents they were in danger. They then grabbed the laptop, stuffed it into one of the bags and sprinted towards the attic's roof access door, and bounded out into the darkness and along the walkway leading to the end of the house. A metal ladder attached to the side of the building jutted up just above the roof's gutter. Using it, they both made their way to the ground and crouched in silence as sounds of alarm blared from the house. Shots rang out a few seconds later indicating a gun battle was raging. Matt pointed to a stand of trees lining the electrified metal fence and both men sprinted towards it.

The compound, consisting of approximately ten acres, was alive with activity and Matt, looking back, saw the two limousines racing towards the entrance. He could also see silhouettes of men spreading out across the compound. Soon they would be heading in their direction.

The stand of trees ran along the fence-line for approximately a quarter mile. Both men surveyed the ones they were standing near, picked a likely candidate and proceeded to climb to the height of the fence. Matt, knowing they would be alright if they didn't ground themselves, dove for the top railing, making sure he cleared any branches that may reach out and touch him. He then jumped to the ground outside of the compound. Vern, tossing the duffle bag to Matt on the other side of the fence, followed suit. Vern then proceeded to take the lead, knowing the approximate direction to where the boat he had prepared ahead of time should be docked. It was approximately a mile from where they were as the crow flies, but they weren't crows! So he took the most direct route he could think of. As they were about to enter the neighborhoods they peered back and saw two sets of ATV lights heading towards their position, men in black hanging all over them!

"How far do we have Vern?

"Not far now; the dock is a half block north of here. We should be able to make it before they catch up with us. I don't think they've seen us yet."

Just as he said that, a shot rang out and hit the side of the house they were next to.

"I'm thinking you're wrong about that one Vern!", and they both sprinted beyond the houses that lined the shoreline and towards the dock. "Which boat is it?"

"The 27 foot utility boat; the red and white one. You release the front line and I'll get the stern. It can go from zero to fifty in three seconds. I'll take the helm; you break out the arsenal. They're in the right storage bin. Hurry, I can see the ATV's coming up the beach about three hundred yards away."

Vern released the back line and jumped the railing. The key was in the ignition just as he had instructed. It started on the first turn of the key and push of the starter button. Matt had released the bow line and jumped aboard, then worked his way back to the storage bins. They were just pulling away from the dock when shots rang out! One hit the windshield just in front of Vern and others riddled the interior. Matt found a couple of M-16s and some clips; he began returning fire. One of the ATV's exploded as a round of Matt's found its gas tank. Bodies flew every which way. The other ATV, being diverted by the blast, turned and slowly drove back in the direction from which it had come.

Matt made his way to where Vern was, "That was a close call Jarhead!"

"Close calls are what we're all about Gunny!"

CHAPTER 16

When they arrived back at their hotel suite the CIA was waiting for them. It was reported that all three of the CIA agents who were working undercover as the catering services were missing. Local law enforcement did not find any bodies or evidence they could use to pursue an investigation of the owners of the estate so they had to leave. A major asset of the operation was the video and audio footage, captured on the laptop, of the guests that had shown up. However, the meeting that Vardon had planned to have did not materialize as a result of Matt and Vern's presence being made known. The CIA, however, concluded that their identities had not been compromised. That was good news! And the plan was to continue shadowing Vardon and see what action he was going to take as a result of not being able to hold that meeting. It was abundantly clear that Vardon's business associates covered the globe and that they were not friendly to the U.S.. Their interests and actions would have worldwide implications not consistent with the United State's. And how did SafePhoto-RD play into this plan, or did it? It was up to Matt to find out what those interests were and how they might impact the United States. It was pretty unlikely that photo radar was involved, considering who those men were; time would tell.

After the CIA left Matt turned to Vern, "You know Vern, that was a close call. I'm thinking this job might lead me to places and situations similar to what we just went through. I can't ask you to go any further in pursuing Vardon. It's too dangerous and I'm not sure I'll even come out of this alive."

"Well isn't that just sweet! As if you could do anything about me leaving a mission before it's completed, you self-righteous ass! Besides, Majors don't give orders to Lieutenant Colonels. Didn't you learn anything in the Corp, you grunt!?"

Matt smiled, "Ok, come along and get your butt shot off if you want, but don't say I didn't give you a chance to bail out."

The next few days were spent trying to find out what Vardon was planning for his next move. They enlisted the CIA to get into Vardon's office and plant a bug. They also requisitioned from the CIA an agent who could read lips and had him view a monitor that increased the resolution of what their telephoto lens was picking up while focused on Vardon's office. It seemed as though Vardon was commanded to pursue another meeting with the same men, but this time he was to hold the meeting in Turkey!

Arrangements were being made and he was to leave in two days. A private jet would fly him from JFK airport to Ataturk airport outside of Istanbul.

Matt and Vern's papers were prepared and expedited through diplomatic channels, courtesy of the CIA. They would also be flying in a private jet but landing an hour prior to Vardon. This would allow them to tail him to where he was planning to meet. A CIA operative in Istanbul would be their guide and chauffer; his undercover name was Derin Sadik. They would identify him by saying 'Loyalty is good', and he was to respond with 'it is the meaning of my name'.

When they arrived at Ataturk airport in Turkey, Derin was holding up a placard that read 'AIC Convention'. Matt and Vern greeted him and confirmed that it was truly their CIA contact. Matt then remarked how inscrutable it was of Derin to use the reverse of 'CIA' on his sign; it drew a broad smile from Derin!

They then drove to where Derin said Vardon's limo was parked, and while they waited discussed their plans. In less than an hour Vardon showed up in a golf cart and transferred to his limousine. They followed him to the 'Marmara Taksim Hotel' in the center of Istanbul, where Vern followed him up in the elevator to the eighteenth floor, which housed the Grand Suites. They then checked into the hotel, eliciting one of the Grand Suites, and found that their room was the fourth one from Vardon's. Stationing Derin in the lobby, to notify them whenever Vardon exited the elevators, they reconnoitered their surroundings; their room, hallway and all possible exits. It was up to Vardon now to make the next move.

CHAPTER 17

Vardon's room had been prepared for him in anticipation of his arrival. In the middle of the suite was a large round table and on it were a dozen 'burner' phones; ones that could not be traced if used once and then destroyed. His main objective at this point was to notify each of the men who were waiting, somewhere in Istanbul, for his call as to where they would meet. In this way, no one could know in advance of the exact meeting place, assuring there would be no outside interference this time. Only Vardon and the other six men would be privy to that information, just before the meeting was to take place. He placed the calls and the meeting was set!

Derin was sitting in the lobby of the hotel pretending to read a paper when Vardon stepped out of the elevator. Derin pushed a button on his cell phone which immediately called Matt's phone, "He just exited the elevator and is moving across the lobby towards the bar. I'll follow him and keep my phone on."

Matt replied, "No Derin, wait for us," but Derin had already placed his phone in his coat pocket and was slowly moving towards the location he had last seen Vardon.

When Derin caught sight of Vardon, Vardon turned towards him and Derin moved off in another direction which took him towards a handsome looking woman who had just entered his line of sight. She moved with an athletic step to her gait; very controlled and powerful. When the two of them passed each other, she brushed against Derin's arm with a gloved hand and then moved on towards Vardon.

Derin felt a slight itching sensation on his arm but turned and went towards the front desk. This allowed him to keep a peripheral view of Vardon, who moved towards the lady and greeted her. They then both moved off towards the front entry doors, indicating they were leaving the hotel.

Matt and Vern were just exiting the elevator when they caught sight of Derin who looked as though he was staggering towards the entryway doors. They rushed towards him and just as Derin reached the sidewalk, he saw Vardon and the girl get into an exotic looking car that had been waiting for them. He turned towards Matt and pointed towards the car, then collapsed to the ground.

Vern immediately started hailing a cab while Matt bent down at Derin's side to see if he could help. Derin looked up at Matt, smiled and then whispered, "AIC Convention, pretty good eh?" and then, with a smile on his face, he closed his eyes. He was dead.

Vern yelled at Matt, "Let's go, they're getting away."

Matt, knowing there was nothing else he could do for Derin, ran for the cab and they sped off in the direction Vardon and the girl had gone. The road led towards a working class district of Istanbul called 'Kagithane', at which point they caught a glimpse of Vardon's car. They told the driver to pull over and at gun point confiscated the cab, leaving the driver on the side of the road and speeding off in pursuit of Vardon.

The highway led them out of the city onto a long road leading northeast. They were definitely out in the desert, with very few buildings in sight, and it was just turning from twilight to dusk. They could see the taillights of Vardon's car out in the distance about a half mile. Afraid their headlights would give them away they shut them off. Another ten minutes and they saw Vardon's car turn east towards what appeared to be a small factory, whose lights could be seen for some distance. All of a sudden Vardon's car lights went off. Matt slowed the cab to a stop and waited for a minute, then drove off the road and into the desert a few hundred yards. It was totally dark now except for the light from the moon.

"We need to leave the car here and proceed on foot, agreed?"

Vern looked at Matt and responded, "Agreed. Let's stagger our approach. When we get back to the road I'll proceed up the left side and you proceed laterally to me up the right. At the first sign of life we drop. When we reach the building, we'll move in the same direction; me to the left and you to the right. I'll call your phone now and we'll keep them turned on to communicate."

It took them ten minutes to reach the building, Matt moving off to the right and Vern to the left and behind the building. It was dark now and only the lights of the building revealed the details of its surroundings to the two men.

Matt found a metal pipe running down the side of the building. Using it as a rope he made his way up to a ledge that ran below some windows on the second floor. He proceeded along the ledge, hugging the building as he went, until he reached the first window which was locked. He continued along the ledge until he found a window that had been left ajar and was about to access the building when he heard cars coming towards the building. Quickly he pried open the window and lifted himself up and through it onto a landing that ran along the inside of a huge warehouse like room. He turned and peered out the window, concealing himself as best he could. Four Hummers pulled up to the building's entryway. Armed men began exiting them and proceeded to surround the building. In the darkness of the night, off in the distance, Matt could see a caravan of cars approaching the building. Just as he caught sight of the cars he heard a door open to the huge room below him and he immediately dropped to the floor of the walkway and began moving himself slowly, inch by inch towards the end of the room, towards the door.

Men entered the huge room where Matt lay concealed above them on the walkway. He had just about made it to the end of the walkway, just adjacent to the door that the men had used to enter the room, when one of them switched on the lights. Matt froze!

The men searched the room below and after a few minutes shut the lights off and exited from the same door they had entered.

He moved to the end of the walkway and used a small wall ladder to access the dark room below. Slowly, he opened the door just enough to see inside the next room and found it to be dark and empty. It was much smaller with desks that had computer monitors on them. He made his way to the other side of the room where he could see another door that led into the interior of the building. Just as he reached for the handle of the door it started to open towards him! He moved with the motion of the door, concealing himself from the guard. As it shut Matt reached for his knife, took one long stride towards the back of him, and with one motion pushed the guards head forward with his left hand while his right hand slid the knife across the guard's throat. The forward movement of the guard precipitated by the push from Matt almost severed his head from its body, which crumpled to the floor lifeless!

Matt grabbed the feet of the guard and dragged the body behind a desk, then moved swiftly back to the door and cautiously cracked it open an inch. The room was filled with men, some sitting at a large table while others were milling around talking to each other. It was obvious to him that this is where the meeting was going to be held and he needed to position himself so he could hear what was being said. He quickly moved to another door that accessed a room next to his. Looking around, he found an air return that was servicing the room the meeting was being held in. He quietly pried off the vent face and opened the opposing vent, allowing him to hear the proceedings.

Matt crouched in the darkness for a few minutes next to the vent, waiting for the meeting to begin, when he heard a muffled sound emanating from his pocket. It was coming from his phone!

"Vern, where are you?"

133

"I ran into some trouble. I've been trying to get you."

"Are you alright?"

"Yes but I had to kill a couple of guards in the back of the building and I'm worried that they'll be missed. Where are you?"

"The meeting is about to begin. Did you conceal the bodies?"

"Yes. They won't be found but sooner or later they will be missed."

"Ok, get back to the car. Disable their vehicles if you can and wait for me about a quarter mile down the road. When the meeting is over I'll make my way there."

"Roger," and Vern hung up.

"Gentlemen, let us begin our meeting please."

It was Vardon who called the meeting to order.

"We all know each other so I will not take up our valuable time with such formalities. Triad-XB is in the business of weaponry, drugs, and intelligence. Each of you represent an interested party within your governments relative to the project known as 'Kathairo'. This meeting is to update you on its progress, assure you of its success and determine at this point who will be the highest bidder of the final product. We are in the last phase of testing. So far we have had a ninety-eight percent success rate utilizing a test base of three hundred subjects. Most of our testing has been done appropriating indigenous subjects found in South America; ones that few miss when destroyed. You might say it is a 'cleansing' or purification process, or 'kathairo'. The electromagnetic radiation laser is now in the process of being designed to attach to a low orbiting satellite, where it can be precisely pointed at a target that is no more than two thousand kilometers away. The target may be as small as five hundred millimeters in length or as wide as one half kilometer! Each of your countries has such satellite technology, making this a viable weapon that is totally undetectable. My company will demonstrate it in a 'real world' environment to the highest bidder. You will select a single subject that fits within those parameters who will then be tracked and destroyed. Complete video monitoring will be provided by us to a select audience consisting of no more than ten spectators. So that all of the non-winners may be aware, the demonstration will take place no more than sixty days from today. Since this is a weapon extraordinaire we will begin the bidding at five million Euros. Bidding will be silent and the winner will be notified incognito so that no one will know exactly which country is in possession of such a weapon; only the winner will know."

Matt had heard all that he needed at this point. The whereabouts of Triad-XB would not be disclosed at this meeting. Those in attendance were the same ones identified at the previous meeting. He now needed to get out of there with this information. Just as he was about to leave, guards rushed into the meeting room announcing they had found one of the guards that had been killed. Matt ran back to where he had come in, climbed up to the open window and exited the building in the same manner he had come. He began running down the road to where Vern was suppose to be waiting for him, quietly calling out his name but to no avail. He figured he had run almost a half mile when all of a sudden he heard a horn honk; it was Vern!

"You had me scared there for a minute buddy."

Vern smiled and his white teeth glimmered in the moonlight, "What! You think I'd left you or something? Only a low ranking Major would think something like that! Did you get any intel we can use?"

"More than we bargained for. I think we have a major task ahead of us that will definitely take all the resources of the CIA, and possibly some we'll need to call in as well."

As they drove back to Istanbul Matt briefed Vern on the information he had acquired relative to the 'Kathairo' project and called their back-up contact to get them a flight back to the states.

When they arrived at the hotel in Istanbul they began gathering up their stuff to leave for the airport. Matt needed to track Vardon, so he covertly broke into Vardon's room and planted two tracking device buttons; one in his laptop and another in his luggage bag. When he picked up the laptop he noticed a mini flash drive still plugged into one of the USB ports. He removed it, rushed back to his hotel room and copied it onto his laptop, hoping it would provide them with information regarding the meeting. He then went back to Vardon's room and replaced the flash drive. He was moving towards the door when he heard the click of the keycard in the door's lock! He drew his gun, stepped through the bathroom door that was behind the main entryway door and froze, hoping Vardon would move into the main room. He did. As the entryway door was shutting Matt grabbed it and exited into the hallway without Vardon seeing him. He then casually walked back to his hotel room where Vern was waiting.

"I think we won't be needing that flight back to the states", Vern said as Matt entered.

"What do you mean?"

"I just finished looking at the data we took off that flash drive of Vardon's; it pertains exclusively to the Kathairo project. It indicates that the R & D and testing location of the project is in Niger, West Africa!"

Matt looked at Vern for a long moment then said, "Let's call Harris and brief him; let him know we're headed to Niger instead of returning. We need to find the location of that project and see how much damage we can do."

CHAPTER 18

Sixteen hours and thirteen hundred miles later, with the help of the CIA and a jet it had supplied, Matt and Vern were disembarking at the Agadez airport in Niger. Their mission, sanctioned by the CIA, was to try and obtain the data and plans for the electromagnetic radiation weapon, or EMR, that was being tested then destroy the weapon and test facilities. Two operatives, who had been flown in from Kano, Nigeria met them at the airport and drove them to a safe house on the outskirts of Agadez. The operatives immediately went to work laying out the ordinances they had brought and assembling two RQ-11 Raven drones to be used for reconnaissance.

Matt opened his laptop and accessed the data he had copied from Vardon's flash drive. It supplied them with a map of the area and the location of the facility, which lay approximately twenty miles from town. As soon as the drones were assembled they were loaded into a tarp-covered truck and the four men were off. They headed west south west along road N11 towards a preserve that had been closed by order of the local Sultan, which was evidently being used to hide the testing facility. As they approached the entry to the preserve they saw that it was being guarded by a small group of men, so they continued on past for approximately two miles. At that point they drove off the road and into the bush, looking for a small clearing from which to launch the drones. As soon as they could they set up a small camp deep in the bush and launched a drone, pointing it towards where the test compound should be. It had a range of a little over six miles; three out and three back. At about one and a half miles out the drone flashed back video of the compound taken from a height of two hundred fifty feet. With the help of the video, and Vardon's data files, Matt and Vern planned their attack. It was a little past noon so they decided to establish a pathway to the compound and then wait for early morning to make their move. It was the weekend so the compound was practically empty of workers; only the garrison of guards would be present.

"Ok, let's gather round and discuss tomorrow's strategy", Matt said to the group. "The plans show that the compound is divided into three sections; one for housing the guards, the other for supplies and heavy equipment, and the third to prepare the weapon for testing, general diagnostics and data gathering. Each section has its own distinct generator system to supply power. From the video supplied by the drone today it looks like there's about fifteen to twenty guards, each heavily armed. Our first objective is to neutralize the perimeter guards without warning the others at the entry to the preserve, which is about a quarter mile from the compound. Any ideas?"

"If I might interject a thought at this point?," said one of the operatives. "This whole area, as well as Nigeria where we've been stationed, mines uranium, silver and gold. As a result we've found that carrying a small supply of potassium cyanide with us, which is used in the manufacturing of these resources, comes in handy. Hence we brought some with us. If we were able to drop some in a couple of containers of water where the guards sleep, the fumes created would eliminate some of them quietly and without disturbing the others."

"Excellent idea", said Vern. "This will necessitate moving our timetable up somewhat so that we catch most of them while they're still sleeping. Say seven hours from now, or 0400 hours. This would allow us time to cut through the perimeter fence and position ourselves within the compound to take out the other guards. We need to use our knives and silencers as much as possible to limit the sound of gunfire. We all have silencers so let's prepare our handguns accordingly. Use your TAR-21's only if a major assault is imminent. We'll each take six thirty-round clips just as a precaution. Each of us will mount a 40 millimeter grenade launcher and carry five grenades for a 'worst case' scenario. Matt, you'll take the EMR weapon section, gather up as much intel as you can and plant three C4 charges to destroy the building and its contents. Set the charges to go off at 0600 hours. We'll all meet back at the perimeter fence where we initially breached it at 0530 hours. That will give us enough time to get back to our truck and be out on the road when the charges go off. We cannot leave any of the guards alive, is that understood? Matt, any thoughts?"

"I think our most exposure will be not knowing exactly where the perimeter guards are going to be when we begin the attack. Hence, I propose two of us be tasked to eliminate that exposure. I'll move to the EMR weapons building and take out any guards that I may run into. At the same time the potassium cyanide will be deployed, with whatever guards not immediately affected being eliminated directly. Its 2100 hours now so let's get prepared; get some sleep and be ready to move out at 0400 hours."

"Check. Let's go," said Vern and they all moved off to prepare themselves for the coming night and impending attack the next morning.

CHAPTER 19

"Mr. Vardon, the helicopter is waiting for your instructions. Do you want me to let them know when you'll arrive?"

"Tell them our plane will touch down in Agadez at 0500 hours and they should be prepared to lift off for the compound immediately upon my arrival, do you understand?"

"Yes sir", said the man who was in command at the EMR weapons compound. He was sitting at his desk in a small room built within the barracks section of the compound; a short wave radio was in front of him. He heard the click at the other end of the receiver as Vardon hung up on him. He immediately contacted the helicopter pilot who was waiting at the Agadez airport and conveyed Vardon's instructions, then turned off the radio. It was late, and he needed to make a final inspection of the compound before he turned in for the night. It would be a long night to say the least. He always got nervous when he knew the big bosses would be arriving and it was difficult for him to sleep. Maybe this time it would be different. Maybe he could finally get some sleep. He would have a few drinks before he went to bed; maybe that would calm his nerves!

Vardon had finished his assignment in Istanbul. The representatives of the various governments had returned to their respective countries and had finalized their bids for the EMR weapon. As a result of the breach at the meeting where a number of the guards had been killed, two of the countries decided to opt out of the bidding process. Never-the-less, the highest bid came in at nine million Euros from the representative of North Korea! Vardon was now waiting word that one third of the funds had been wired to Triad-XB's offshore bank accounts, and a communiqué from North Korea indicating the specific 'test target' they wanted destroyed so as to show the weapon's effectiveness. He was now on his way to visit the compound and prepare to have the weapon shipped to be installed on a satellite that Triad-XB owned, under the guise of one of their communication companies in Europe.

Vardon touched down in Agadez at five in the morning and the helicopter was waiting for him. Before he left the plane he received a call from 'home plate'; the code name that identified the headquarters of Triad-XB. The money had been deposited by North Korea and the target had been identified. It was the U.S. embassy in Japan! The logic behind the target was to destabilize the feelings of the American people relative to the nuclear plants that had been destroyed and the propaganda being fed to them that the threat had been neutralized, and stability was returning to the Japanese economy. It would also provide an object lesson to Japan for future negotiations relative to the North China sea and Japan's insistence that the major trade route, the Strait of Malacca, belonged to them.   The strait links the Indian and Pacific Oceans and facilitates the movement of approximately 25% of all traded goods in that part of the world. It also carries approximately 25% of all oil that travels by sea. At its narrowest point, just south of Singapore, the Strait of Malacca is only 1.5 nautical miles wide, making it one of the world's most noteworthy strategic chokepoints. China and North Korea needed to control that area, and with Japan's current hold on it that could not happen.

The target pleased Vardon and he couldn't wait to get to the compound to set things in motion, excited to finally think the weapon would no longer be wasted on meaningless 'guinea pigs'!

****

Matt, Vern and their two CIA operatives reached the compound's perimeter fence at 0430 hours. At 0500 hours they had 'neutralized' the perimeter's guards and the potassium cyanide gas had just been deployed in the barracks. It would only take ten minutes and the remaining guards would be dead.

Matt was at the EMR weapons building, and had just finished neutralizing a guard when he though he heard the faint sound of a helicopter. A computer station was surrounded by various cargo containers which held crated boxes ready for shipment; probably the weapon itself. One of the cargo containers was being used for a makeshift office. He moved to the computer station and started to access the operating system. A small device the CIA had supplied to him was inserted into one of the computer's USB ports. When the system booted up it was taken over by the programs on the device and all the data was downloaded. In the process a worm was installed onto the system that would infiltrate any network that may be accessed. Matt extracted the device when the download was completed and placed it in a compartment hidden under the heel of one of his shoes; another device the CIA had provided. Just as he was finishing, Vern came into the building and moved swiftly towards Matt.

"We need to get out of here, now! A helicopter is landing and it looks like it's loaded with unfriendlies. Have you placed the charges?"

"No, I just finished getting the data off the hard drive. The explosives are in the bag; get to it. I want to check out that cargo carrier over there then I'll meet you at the door."

"Don't take too long. I stationed the two CIA operatives to cover our exit."

Matt ran to the container that was set up as an office while Vern began placing the C4 charges. At the back of the container Matt found another small room that was partitioned off from the front portion by a metal 'floor to ceiling' gate. It was dark so he couldn't see inside the small room. He flashed a light on the gate and found it was locked. As he did so he thought he saw a movement on the other side. When he pointed his light into the room he was shocked!

"Matt, the charges are placed. We have two minutes to get out of here. Let's get....", and Vern caught site of what Matt was staring at.

Behind the locked gate, crouched down in the corner of the cargo container, were three young girls!

"Get back...", and Matt pulled the pistol from its holster located beneath his coat. He stepped back and pulled the trigger two times; the lock exploded into pieces. He grabbed the gate door and he and Vern moved inside, each grabbing one of the girls. Vern grabbed the hand of the other and all five of them ran for the station's door. Just as they exited the building the concussion of the blasts knocked them off their feet and into the bush.

Gunfire rang out as Matt, Vern and the girls recovered from their ordeal. The three girls ran off further into the bush surrounding the buildings. Matt and Vern couldn't do anything about the girls so they ran towards the perimeter fence, hoping their CIA operatives would be waiting. It was light now and they could see where the helicopter had landed. It was almost obscured from their sight due to the dense bush surrounding them. They found the hole in the fence they had used earlier, but no sign of their CIA operatives. They couldn't wait. They had to get out of there and on the road before it was cut off by the entryway guards, so they sprinted down the path towards their truck. When they saw the truck it looked like their operatives were there waiting for them, but something didn't look right. As they approached the truck Vern went to the front and Matt went to the back. As Matt came around the back he could see the legs of one of the operatives dangling from the bed of the truck. When he rounded the corner and looked in the operative's body was in a sitting position. His torso was tied to the inside of the truck. His head was sitting in his lap!

"Matt...come here quick!"

Matt went to the cab of the truck from where Vern had called him. He saw the other CIA operative's body slouched over the steering wheel. Stab wounds riddled his body, and his throat had been cut from ear to ear.

"The guards at the front gate must have been waiting for them," Vern broke the silence. "Let's get out of here before they come back."

Matt grabbed the body of the man in the cab and jerked it out and onto the ground, then jumped in behind the steering wheel. Vern was already in and closing the door when the first missile from the helicopter hit the ground in front of them! A massive explosion followed, blowing the front windshield out of the truck and lifting it up off the ground. Matt started the truck, put the pedal to the floorboard, and popped the clutch; they were off!

The helicopter carried Vardon and a crew of four, each of which was heavily armed. It maneuvered around in the air for another shot at the truck but it was too late. The truck had disappeared into the bush under the canopy of the trees and onto the path heading towards the road.

Vern, sitting next to Matt in the truck, zipped the tarp that separated the cab from the back and went through. He grabbed one of the RPK machine guns that the CIA had provided, shoved a 45 round magazine into it and moved to the back of the truck to wait for a sighting of the helicopter.

Matt moved the truck onto the highway leading back towards Agadez. He had traveled about a mile when the helicopter came into view. It was headed straight for them. As it approached he could see two individuals leaning out of its sides, their guns pointed at the truck.

"Vern", Matt yelled, "they're heading straight at us. When I yell 'now' be prepared to fire. I'm going to spin the truck around, got it?"

"Got it", yelled Vern.

The helicopter was hovering now, above the highway out in front of them. As Matt came closer he yelled 'NOW', hit the brakes and turned the steering wheel, spinning the truck around so Vern was facing the helicopter.

The two men in the helicopter started firing their weapons at the truck as it began its reversal of direction, but their bullets crashed into the pavement next to it.

Vern had the advantage now as he was in an excellent position; he opened up and the RPK machine gun spewed its fire and bullets at the helicopter. He could see the bullets hit the side of the chopper, then take out one of the men who had been firing at him.

"Get out of here", yelled Vardon to the helicopter pilot. "We're sitting ducks, you bungling idiot. Get back to the airport as soon as possible. I must return to Istanbul as soon as possible."

Matt put the truck in gear and turned it back towards Agadez, as Vern untied the dead CIA operative and pushed his body out of the truck. He then made his way back to the cab.

"That was a close one gunny."

"What, you wanna be a barracks rat Major. Afraid of a little action?"

"No colonel, but I don't relish the idea of making this place my 'final duty station' either! That was good shooting. Keep it up and I'll have to recommend they give you some chest candy for this mission. You brass love that stuff don't you?"

Vern grinned at Matt with his bright white teeth, "Yes we do. And I'll take all I can get; the women love it!"

On the way back to the safe house outside Agadez Matt and Vern planned their next move. They needed to report in to the CIA that the prototype of the weapon had been destroyed, along with the compound, and turn over the data they had acquired from the computer. A major concern was how they would find out where the weapon would be used and by whom; what country had won the lottery. They came to the conclusion that the only person who had that information was Vardon so they needed to follow him and find a way to obtain it. They called in their report, downloaded the data to Langley and asked if the CIA could find out where Vardon's jet was headed. Their jet was waiting for them at the Agadez airport and took off immediately upon their arrival. It was back to Istanbul, and Vardon had a two hour head start. The pilot was instructed to make up as much time as he could and Langley had notified an operative in Istanbul to wait for Vardon's jet and tail him, then report to Matt at the Marmara Taksim Hotel.

****

Vardon's plans needed to change now that the testing facility had been destroyed along with one of the prototypes of the weapon. The plant, just outside of Istanbul where the weapon was manufactured, needed to have security beefed up as well as within the city. The timetable for deployment of the weapon needed to be moved forward so the North Koreans would continue to have faith in the project, just in case they found out about the destruction of the testing plant. Another means of delivery needed to be devised so as to eliminate the necessity of installing it on the satellite; that could be accomplished by the North Koreans once they owned the plans and the project had come to a successful conclusion. Of course it was the CIA who had found out about the testing facility but who were the two men who had gotten away? What had they found out before they destroyed the facility? How could it be used to thwart his plans? He needed to get back to Istanbul and get the weapon readied for deployment no matter what the cost!

CHAPTER 20

Once Matt had set up camp back at the Marmara Taksim Hotel in Istanbul and found out Vardon had returned to his facilities outside the city he and Vern tasked a number of operatives to maintain a vigil over the place. Three days after their return two large flatbed trucks carrying shipping containers arrived and proceeded to Vardon's facility. The CIA watched as the cargo within the containers was unloaded; the cargo was Cheyenne helicopter parts! Then, a few days later, they left the facility and proceeded to the airport where they were loaded onto a C-5 Galaxy cargo plane.

The CIA was notified and directed one of its satellites to follow the plane and pinpoint its destination. It took off the next day and landed in Pakistan fourteen hours later. It refueled then proceeded on, heading out over mainland China towards North Korea. The final destination was a small island off the coast of North Korea called Al-som, located in the Sea of Japan. It had been readied by the North Korean's for the landing of such a plane. Satellite pictures showed the containers being emptied of their contents. They were of two Cheyenne helicopters being off-loaded into a large metal structure at the northeast end of the island. The Cheyenne has a range of over a thousand miles and an air speed of close to two hundred and fifty.

With North Korea's two new naval frigates, designed specifically for helicopters, a covert attack on the interior of Japan or South Korea would now be possible. Matt was sure that the helicopters, shipped to Istanbul in cargo containers to Vardon's facilities, had been equipped with the EMR weapon! And knowing that Japan and South Korea had the Cheyenne as their primary helicopter it would be easy for North Korea to get within striking distance of either country's interior cities!

CHAPTER 21

Major General Jin-ho of the North Korean army had been tasked by General Sung-min to work with Vardon in planning the 'demonstration' of the EMR weapon, once the bidding was over.

North Korea's relations with the United States, and its mortal enemy Japan, had always been described as a 'simmering' one. But with North Korea's continued insistence on developing nuclear weapons and long-range missiles it escalated to the boiling point when, in 2010, North Korea torpedoed a South Korean warship. The DPRK was committed to pushing the two powers to their breaking point and an attack from an 'unknown' entity upon Japan at this point in time would hopefully accomplish that goal.

"Jin-ho, the General of the Army has directed me to change the target; the U.S. Embassy in Tokyo is no longer the objective. Sources within Japan have disclosed that in eight days a secret meeting will take place that will include Japan's Deputy Prime Minister, Minister of Defense and Minister of Ocean Policy. It will take place on one of their newly commissioned Destroyers, the 'Atago', moored near Matsue, Japan. That will be the new target!" General Sung-min handed Jin-ho a folder that contained the details necessary for him to accomplish the task. "Do you have any questions Major?"

"No General, I will review the information, meet with Mr. Vardon and plan the attack. It shall be accomplished!" As soon as Jin-ho finished with General Sung-min he reached into an inside pocket of his coat and retrieved a phone. He pushed a button and it called a predefined number; a voice on the other end answered, "Agent Harris here". Jin-ho quickly conveyed to Agent Harris the plans he had just discussed with General Sung-min and told him they need to act immediately!

Agent Harris called Matt and told him the information he had obtained from Jin-ho: "Matt, I'm readying a plane for you as we speak. You and Vern will be flying from Istanbul to Nagasaki tonight to develop a plan with the Japanese to stop Vardon from succeeding. Keep me posted on your progress and let me know if you need anything. If at all possible see if you can get Vardon; he is now officially an enemy of the U.S."

CHAPTER 22

Matt and Vern arrived in Nagasaki and were greeted by Colonel Akio of the Japanese Air Self-Defense. They then traveled to a small military base located ten kilometers from where the 'Atago' was moored. Matt reviewed everything he knew about the mission with the Colonel; that it would be carried out by Vardon and the North Koreans from the island of Al-som, located in the Sea of Japan. A Cheyenne helicopter with South Korean markings would take off from Al-som within a few days armed with an Electromagnetic Radiation weapon, focused on destroying the Japanese officials that would be on board the Atago. He asked the Colonel to provide him with a hand held FIM-92 Stinger RMP surface to air missile and to task a satellite to watch over the island of Al-som in order to know exactly when Vardon's helicopter left for its mission. He told the Colonel that an undercover agent within the ranks of the North Korean army would be contacting Matt with the exact time of the attack and that Matt would need to be 'out to sea' when the Atago reached its destination point. He would need to be told when Vardon's helicopter was within range of the missile he would be carrying and that the Atago should prepare for a 'worst case' scenario in the event his plan failed. The

Colonel followed his recommendations and provided Matt with an extremely fast, long range Interceptor M-46 motor boat that was difficult for radar to detect in the open seas. Vern would be driving and Matt would man the missile. The Atago would be tasked to stay within a hundred miles of the coast, thus allowing the interceptor plenty of leeway to do its job and return safely to shore if needed.

From Vardon's island of Al-som, Matsue was approximately 450 miles. With the Atago being 100 miles off the shoreline of Japan, it meant Vardon's striking distance would be less than 400 miles, or a two hour flight at most. Matt had reviewed the plans they had taken from Vardon's warehouse in Niger and knew that the weapon had to be within a horizontal distance of no more than twenty five miles of its target. Since the Cheyenne's service ceiling was twenty thousand feet Matt calculated he would have to be at least twenty miles west of the Atago when he fired his missile since it had a maximum range of five miles. There would be no room for errors.

Vardon made contact with Jin-ho and directed him to gather whoever was going to watch the demo and fly to the island of Al-som in two days to prepare to witness the demonstration. The delegation was selected by Jin-ho and flown to the island where Vardon was waiting to greet them. He then directed the group to a conference hall for a briefing.

"Gentlemen, the demonstration will take place tomorrow night at 1600 hours. We're readying the equipment as we speak. The weapon will be delivered to the site by a Cheyenne helicopter with markings that simulate a South Korean aircraft. I am sure Major Jin-ho has filled you in on the target so I will dispense with that part of my speech. The helicopter is equipped with multiple cameras that will provide you with wide angle as well as telephoto shots of the occurrence as it happens. Since we will not actually see the demise of any of the occupants within the ship, all of whom will be completely destroyed, we will see the effect of the weapon on those who are on deck and within view of the cameras. Any organic item that exists on the ship will be combusted and will, to clarify, explode from within! The electromagnetic radiation pulse will cover the whole ship and will be delivered from a height of ten thousand feet and twenty miles from its target. Once the EMR pulse is initiated it will take approximately thirty seconds to bring the subjects to a boiling point for the combustion to occur. During the first fifteen seconds the subjects will start to feel some discomfort but no damage will have been done. All electrical equipment within the pulse, however, will be disabled. Within the next ten seconds the boiling of fluids will occur and the combustion will follow. Are there any questions?"

Jin-ho waited for a response from his associates and when none was forthcoming he stood, "Mr. Vardon, I have a question, if I may? How do you expect to get within range to fire the weapon without being detected?"

Vardon knew that this was the only weak spot in the plan and peered at Jin-ho for a few seconds before answering: "As I said previously, we have simulated one of South Korea's Cheyenne helicopters down to the air defense identification marks. A flight plan has been filed at the Ulsan airport in South Korea and cleared with Japan. Of course no flight will actually originate from there; we will attack from here. The Japanese will have very little time to verify with South Korea the validity of the helicopter. Confusion will assure that fact. Do you have any other questions, Major?"

Jin-ho bowed slightly, sat down without responding, and the meeting was adjourned. That night Jin-ho made a phone call on a burner phone to a number in South Korea. The call was then routed through two other numbers until it was finally answered: "Agent Harris".

CHAPTER 23

Agent Harris notified Matt as soon as he got off the phone with Jin-ho that Vardon would attack in forty-eight hours! This coincided with the schedule of the Atago which was to leave its base in thirty-six hours. The ship had been prepared for the worst case scenario, or so Matt had been told. The Interceptor M-46 motor boat that Matt and Vern would be using was going to be towed to the one hundred mile site by the Atago. Matt and Vern would board it just before the Atago reached its destination and begin their journey out into the ocean an additional twenty-five miles, then wait for word from the Colonel that the helicopter was fifty miles from their position. This would provide them with approximately ten to twelve minutes before the enemy would be above them at ten thousand feet. They also had a hand held radar detector that was good out to a distance of twenty miles. Their plan was to wait for the Colonel's call, turn on their radar detector, prepare the missile, wait until the helicopter was within four miles of them and fire!

"Gentlemen, please focus on the screen in front of you as we are ready to begin the demonstration", and with that Vardon waived to a man who immediately typed something into a computer and an image of the helicopter flying over the ocean appeared.

"We are approximately forty miles or ten minutes from the Japanese destroyer, the Atago. We are flying at a speed of approximately two hundred-fifty miles per hour at a height of ten thousand feet. In five minutes we will be twenty miles from our target, which you can easily make out a little below the horizon. In two minutes the air speed will begin to be reduced in order to start positioning the craft to fire the weapon. We are now focusing in on the deck of the destroyer where we will find a specific subject to monitor."

Colonel Akio's call to Matt and Vern came at just before four o'clock in the afternoon, and Matt immediately turned on their radar detector. Vern grabbed the long range binoculars and started scouring the western skies overhead and watching the radar screen.

"Got 'em", yelled Vern as he peered at the radar then raised his arm, pointing skyward."

Matt had positioned himself in the boat with the surface to air missile and was preparing it for firing, "Just about ready. How far out does the radar say they are", Matt yelled to Vern.

"Two miles. You can fire any time now, they're within our range."

Matt turned on the missile and it immediately acquired its target. "Cover your ears, here it goes". He pressed the triggering mechanism and the ejection motor fired the missile. The projectile shot up into the sky and within seconds of clearing the boat its solid-fuel rocket motor kicked into gear. Matt immediately loaded it again while the first missile began its journey at mach speed towards the helicopter.

"Gentlemen, I will now initiate the pulse on the weapon. Please focus on the subject and in thirty seconds it will," and Vardon stopped in mid sentence as the monitor everyone was viewing went bright white, then black! He immediately turned to his technician and yelled, "What is going on!"

Vardon's technician checked his control panel and everything was as it should be. He turned to Vardon and said, "Whatever has happened, it has nothing to do with the equipment. It must have happened on board the helicopter. In fact, the equipment indicates that the helicopter no longer exists. I'm not sure what that means sir."

"You stupid idiot. It means it was shot down!" Vardon heard the words coming out of his mouth and stopped himself immediately.

The men in the room stood up and started talking to each other in their native tongue. Major Jin-ho turned to Vardon and said, "This has been a fiasco since the beginning! You failed when the bidding was to take place, you failed when your factory was destroyed, and now you have failed to prove your weapon! We expect an immediate return of our government's down payment to your Triad-X corporation. We're washing our hands of this project Vardon, and expect no further discussions on this matter! Do you understand?"

"Gentlemen, the weapon works! Just because something occurred during the demonstration doesn't mean failure! Let me find out what happened and get back to you. It may have been something to do with the malfunctioning of the helicopter, or a bird sucked into the engine; something as simple as that. Give us a chance to show you that the weapon is real and works. It has proven itself in all of our tests previous to this. I'm sure there is a simple explanation for this unfortunate incident."

Jin-ho stared at him, "You know as well as us that your helicopter and weapon was shot down, just as you said when you yelled it out. Our confidence in you and your project no longer exists. Do not pursue this any further Mr. Vardon, we're finished!"

Vardon's first thought was how to contain the situation. If this fiasco became known to his employer he would be a marked man; no a dead man! He pressed a button on a device he always carried. It was a security precaution that had gotten him out of trouble before. All three doors of the room they were in burst open and armed men rushed in. Vardon yelled, "kill them all"!

His men looked at him for a second then the leader opened fire signaling the others to begin firing as well. In less than ten seconds all of the dignitaries, along with Major Jin-ho, had been slaughtered. Only Vardon and the technician were still alive. Vardon slowly walked over to the technician and placed his hand on his shoulder in a friendly gesture and smiled. He casually reached into his coat pocket, took out a small handgun and shot the man in the temple. He then replaced the gun in its holder, straightened his coat and hair, turned to the leader of the gunmen and said, "Clean this mess up. Take all the bodies to the plane they came in, make sure the crew is on board and blow it up. Make it look like an accident. Make sure the bodies cannot be found riddled with bullets. I want no evidence that this meeting ever took place, do you understand?"

"Yes sir," was the only reply and with that Vardon left the slaughter scene muttering to himself, "Power IS everything!"

Vardon went to his room and made a phone call to his superior, "Sir, something has happened. We were unable to hold the demonstration. The plane that was bringing the North Korean delegation blew up just as it was landing. I suspect foul play and am scouring the island as we speak to determine the cause. I am about to notify the North Koreans of their loss but wanted to report the incident to you first. Yes, everyone on board was killed; no survivors. I will endeavor to negotiate another demonstration but I have a feeling they will try and back out of the deal. From the beginning they were reluctant to cooperate. I will pursue another buyer immediately; one less reluctant."

CHAPTER 24

Matt and Vern had returned to their hotel room in Nagasaki after shooting down the helicopter and destroying the weapon. Matt was contacted by Agent Harris the next day and was told that the satellite tasked to watch Vardon's island had picked up the explosion of the North Korean delegation's airplane. They had been trying to contact Major Jin-so, their agent on the island, but to no avail. It was assumed that Jin-so had also been killed in the explosion and that Vardon was trying to cover up his mistakes.

"Matt, before Vardon is able to leave that island we want you to get over there and neutralize him, and any other weapons he may have shipped there. We'll keep our satellite focused on the island and let you know of any unusual activity. We believe he'll stay there until he has retrofitted another helicopter with that weapon, for another strike or possibly for shipment to another buyer. I've already prepared transportation for you as well as some support. You'll need to approach from the sea and at night. Our operative who is in charge of the support team has all the information you need, as well as weapons. You'll be leaving in two hours. Any questions?"

"No, we'll be ready but are you sure you want us to kill Vardon at this time? It seems he'd be more valuable to us alive if we're going to continue our pursuit of Triad".

"If you can extract any information from him, fine. But the consensus at Langley is to terminate him now. We believe we've found his superior, and Vardon is now expendable. It would be best if it happened outside the U.S., do you understand?"

Matt concurred then hung the phone up and sat for a moment thinking about what he and Vern had gotten themselves into. He understood why the CIA was using them instead of their own agents to run the ground operations; complete deniability if things went sideways and they were caught. The support teams didn't personally know them which meant no attachments in the event of a loss. They were probably being paid out of a 'black box' fund which meant the money couldn't be traced. It was as if they didn't exist as far as the government was concerned. The only people that would miss them would be their own friends and family and for Matt and Vern that meant as many as could be counted on one hand! The CIA had done their homework well by choosing Matt for their missions, but loyalty is a two way street. He had no ties to the CIA; no friends or acquaintenances he couldn't loose. They were as expendable to him as he was to them, and with that thought his whole body seemed to relax. The only other person, besides himself, that he cared about was Vern, and Vern didn't need a babysitter when the going got tough. He picked up the phone and called Vern's hotel room: "Its PCS time in less than two hours. Are you ready to become a 'sugar cookie' grunt? Grab your K-bar and be ready for a 'rubber duck' operation; it looks like we're going to do a 'body snatch'. Let's meet in my room in twenty minutes and I'll bring you up to speed on our next escapade!" Matt heard a 'HooYah' from the other end and hung up. He would truly miss his friend if anything happened to him. He vowed silently to make sure that nothing did, even if it meant loosing his own life. Probably the only person in the world who would miss me, Matt thought, is Ciara. She seemed like worlds away from him right then. Would he ever see her again? Only time would tell.

CHAPTER 25

The CRRC or 'combat rubber raiding craft' Matt was crouched next to in the helicopter was partially inflated and ready to be dropped into the sea. The support team was preparing the craft as Matt stared mindlessly into the darkness below. The shore of the island couldn't be seen since they were five miles from the insertion point. The signal was given, the CRRC was dropped, and one by one each team member jumped from the helicopter into the ocean. Matt and Vern were the last to jump; thumbs up and out they went! It was only a twenty foot drop but it seemed like an eternity until they hit the water then a gut wrenchingly cold slammed him into reality! By the time they reached the raft the support team had made it ready for take off, and as Matt's last leg was hoisted up and into the belly of the craft it surged forward as if it were a raging bull that had just been poked with an electric prod. It reached full speed, or about thirty miles per hour, and in less than ten minutes they shut the motors down to a low hum. The shoreline and cliffs could now be seen in the waning moonlight as the boat glided onto the beach. The crew offloaded all the gear that had been prepared for the mission, pushed the craft back out into the ocean, then it slowly turned and was gone as fast as it had come. Not more than a few minutes had passed since they had landed and the boat could no longer be seen. The next time they would see it Vardon would be dead, if all went as planned! Matt knew that the real work lay just before them and unless everyone did exactly what they were suppose to none of them would survive.

The last satellite images indicated that Vardon and his henchmen had set up their headquarters in one of the airfield's hangars located at the southern most end of the runway, and approximately a half mile from where Matt and his team had landed. On the easterly side of the hangar thirty foot high berms of dirt, covered with vegetation, had been created to protect it from the blowing winds. The team worked it's way from the shoreline up the small embankment of cliffs and onto the tops of the berms.

"Ok, each of you has your assignments. The three of you will neutralize anything outside of the building without giving away our presence, then set up a defensive perimeter. You two will come with us and take care of business on the inside. Set your charges for fifteen minutes once we determine Vardon is in the building. We want to destroy all possible remnants of the weapons he has there as well as any electronics. We'll all meet back here after the job is done. Let's go!" And with that Matt led the small contingent of men in their assault on the targeted building. Only the stars and a small sliver of the moon lit their way.

Vardon's laboratory had been set apart from the rest of the work areas. The equipment that produced the electromagnetic radiation required a large amount of electricity as well as sophisticated chambers to capture magnetic atoms created by specialized scientific tools. He had spared no expense in creating a comfortable atmosphere for himself within the confines of the laboratory. He had decided that this is where he would stay until the project was completed and the weapon had been sold and delivered. Twenty of his best men had been stationed around and within the building. His chief mercenary personally guarded Vardon and carried out his orders from within the lab.

Matt, Vern and the two support team members worked their way towards one of the doors that breached the building; it was being guarded by two mercenaries. The two man support team worked their way towards the guards and when they were twenty feet from the door their silencers belched out muffled chokes of smoke. As the two men slumped silently to the ground the CIA operatives rushed forward and replaced their headgear with the dead guards' gear. They took their positions at the door, just as the guards had been doing prior to their demise. Matt and Vern immediately rushed forward and into the building, followed by the two operatives. The four men worked their way around the interior of the building with Matt indicating to the men the equipment that was to be blown up. They went to work setting their explosive charges as Matt and Vern proceeded towards the door that led into Vardon's lab. They tried opening the door but it was locked. Matt spied what seemed like an air passage opening high up and to the left of the door; crates and boxes were stacked below it. Matt indicated to Vern to guard the door while he tried going up and through the passageway. When he reached the opening and looked in he could barely see what looked like a walkway which lead into the darkness. He took a small pen-light from his pocket and clicked it on. Cautiously he stepped through and onto the walkway, having to bend over slightly so as to miss hitting his head on the ceiling. After going about twenty feet he could see that it ended abruptly, with no way to go but back. A cold chill ran down his spine. He felt as though his stomach was going to be sick; it was a trap! The floor under his feet gave way and the next moment he felt his body loose gravity. It crumpled like a rag doll as it hit a padded floor below. He looked over and grabbed the light he had been holding a second before and panned around the room. A second later a door to the room opened, then closed immediately. Abruptly a beam of light pierced the darkness focusing itself on Matt's face, temporarily blinding him. Then a voice politely announced itself.

"Walk over to the table and place all your weapons on it now, or you will be dead in two seconds."

Matt, still blinded by the light, did as he was told.

Again the voice instructed, "Very good. Now move over to the door and place your back against it with your hands clasped behind you."

As soon as he complied the door opened and Matt's hands were secured from behind with a zip tie, then a hood went over his head. Hands abruptly grabbed his right arm and led him fifty paces into the confines of the lab. When his captor had positioned him, he removed the hood. Matt blinked his eyes a few times to gain orientation and found himself standing in front of Vardon.

"Well, well, the mouse has caught the cat! It wasn't supposed to work out that way was it? Can I assume that it was your actions that brought my helicopter down, before the weapon could be fired?"

"You can assume anything you want Vardon."

"Ah, you know my name? How long have you been following me?"

"Let's just say long enough to know you're out of your element."

This comment brought an angry grin to Vardon's face as he motioned to his henchman with his head, which evidently meant bad Karma for Matt. The guard hit Matt with a karate chop at the base of his neck where it met his shoulder, and Matt went to his knees wreathing in pain.

A sound came from the direction of the room that Matt had been captured in and the guard looked at Vardon, who nodded his head towards the passageway leading to the room. The guard took off in the direction of the noise. Vardon then pulled a gun from his coat and pointed it at Matt, "I don't know who you are, Mr....?" and he waited for a response.

"Bower. Matt Bower. And just for the record, it was I that interrupted both of your meetings with the buyers of your weapon. You see, we've been one step ahead of you all along. You, SafePhoto-RD, and Triad." He was trying to bait Vardon into giving him information on Triad, knowing Vardon's ego had been bruised. He was also trying to buy time in hopes Vern would interrupt the situation by killing Vardon's soldier and making an entrance soon. Matt had been casing the room and its contents as soon as the hood had been removed from his head. He also knew the techniques of getting out of plastic zip tie 'handcuffs' and was ready to make his move. Just then, three shots rang out coming from the direction of where he had been captured. Startled, Vardon took his attention off Matt and looked away. Matt broke the band holding his wrists and hurtled his body, with all his might, to his right and behind a large metal container. He reached down to his ankle and pulled out his concealed DB9 handgun. It only held seven bullets so he knew he had to make every shot count.

Instinctively, without accurately aiming, Vardon pulled the trigger of his gun three times. None of his shots found their mark.

Matt feverishly worked his way around the equipment and onto a metal platform at the back of the laboratory where he found an electrical transformer. The power line feeding it had a quick-release that attached it to the transformer. He tucked his gun in his waistband, grabbed the power line and turned, then pulled; the line came free. He followed the line with his eyes back to the wall and saw where it entered a box with a switch on it. It was in the off position. As he looked, he noticed that the location of the box allowed whoever was working the switch to step off the landing and onto an independent stoop covered with rubber. He bent down and jammed the end of the power line into crevasses of the metal platform he was standing on, made his way back to the box and onto the little stoop, just as Vardon rounded the corner and stepped onto the landing.

Vardon spied Matt crouching down at the back of the room near the wall. "Well, well. Trapped like a rat in a bottle. As I've always said, power IS everything and I now have all the power!" He raised his gun and pointed it at Matt with a satisfied look on his face.

Matt, looking seemingly helpless without his gun, stood up from his crouched position and stared at Vardon, "Be careful of what you ask for Vardon," and with one quick movement of his hand he grabbed the lever of the electrical box and slammed it down!

Vardon's eyes opened wide and his body arched backward, shaking with such fervor that he looked like a rag doll attached to some invisible stick being shaken by a controlled 'unnatural' force.

Matt started to see smoke coming from Vardon's ears and eyes and waited a few more seconds before he switched the power off. He walked over to where Vardon's body now lay stiff as a board on the walkway, looked down at it and said, "The application of the power is more important than just power itself. Sweet dreams!"

Moments later Vern found Matt as they made their way out of the building, reconnoitering with their team at the top of the berms. They looked back out over the hangar they had just come from and waited. In less than ten seconds, with clouds hiding the morning sun, an explosion rocked the ground and the sky glowed brightly over a building that no longer existed. In less than five minutes they had been picked up by the raiding craft and were speeding away from the island towards their rendezvous point; mission accomplished!

CHAPTER 26

A week had passed since Matt's episode with Vardon. Marcy was working on her computer in the entryway office outside his, and he was sitting at his desk reflecting on the time he had spent in Turkey, Niger, Japan and a small Korean island in the China Sea, when his phone buzzed.

"Matt, it's Mr. Lanskey. Want me to transfer it in?"

"Yes Marcy. Any time he calls just transfer him to me."

"Ok boss, will do."

"Manny, how have things been going with the 'SafePhoto' project; any headway yet?"

"Matt. They found me out. I'm being held," and Matt heard the thunder of a gun shot ring out on the other end of the line. After a few seconds of nothing, a man's voice broke the silence.

"Watch your back Bower....your time is about up!", and the phone went dead.

Epilogue

Bower seemed to have accomplished what needed to be done, but at what cost? Both SafePhoto-RD and Triad-XB were still doing business as usual, and a trusted friend of his had been killed. It almost seemed as though he was back at square one, except for the fact that this time people wanted him dead!

www.ingramcontent.com/pod-product-compliance
Lightning Source LLC
Chambersburg PA
CBHW020639180626
46816CB00003B/1044